Flamingos and Murder

A Parker Bell Humorous Mystery

Sharon E. Buck

For more information, or to book an event, contact :

info@sharonebuck.com

http://www.SharonEBuck.com

Cover design by Steven Novak, NovakIllustration.com

First Edition: December, 2022

CONTENTS

1. Chapter 1   1

2. Chapter 2   22

3. Chapter 3   30

4. Chapter 4   34

5. Chapter 5   44

6. Chapter 6   60

7. Chapter 7   63

8. Chapter 8   70

9. Chapter 9   77

10. Chapter 10   84

11. Chapter 11   93

12. Chapter 12   99

13. Chapter 13   105

14. Chapter 14   115

15. Chapter 15   128

16. Chapter 16   148

17. Chapter 17   158

18. Chapter 18   167

19. Chapter 19   177

20. Chapter 20   185

21. Chapter 21   191

22. Chapter 22   194

23. About the Author   196

24. Acknowledgements   198

CHAPTER 1

Good golly, Miss Molly! I ain't never seen her strut her beautiful pink body like that before. Look at her posing. Plus, she's standing on one leg, smiling at my customers, giving them that one slow eye look, and winking at them. You tell me how I'm supposed to compete with that?"

I sighed and glanced at the man standing next to me in the Florida heat and humidity. It was an oh-it's-so-hot-you-could-fry-an-egg-on-the-hood-of-your-car kind of day. Don't laugh, it's totally possible...I've done it.

Did I also mention the humidity was worse than any high-end, upscale sauna I've ever been to? I would gladly pay to be in one of those spa saunas about now because it was way cooler there than it was here on the beautiful St. Johns River near Po'thole, Florida.

The gentleman, and I use that term loosely, standing next to me is everything you think of when someone says, "Florida fish camp owner." He was Florida Gator linebacker large, which he had been way back in the day, was wearing orange and blue flip flops aka the official shoe wear of Floridians and wannabes everywhere, stained beige cargo shorts, and, of course, a very loud shirt.

What did his shirt look like? I'm glad you asked...and feel free to roll your eyes...it was an open neck button shirt with an orange background with blue and light green palm fronds, a couple of official logo Florida Gator heads, and, for good measure, a liberal sprinkling of flamingos dancing their way across the shirt. To say it was loud was a massive understatement; however, it's Florida and what can I say about the fashion couture of a small, sleepy, rural Southern town. You're never going to see one of our kind gracing the runway during New York City's Fashion Week.

Horace Bailey Skinner was putting a pinch of dip between his cheek and gum. A very nasty habit as far as I was concerned and, suffice it to say, he and I would never be dating.

"Yep, Miss Maisy certainly knows how to make my customers pay attention to her."

Rolling my eyes and trying hard not to laugh while rivers of salty water were running down my face, "You know Miss Maisy is one of the reasons why people come here to eat, don't you?"

He grinned. He was barely sweating. I think I hate him. "Hubba Bubba's Fish Camp will do anything to bring in the customers."

Yes, ladies and gentlemen, Horace Bailey Skinner is known as Hubba Bubba. Apparently, he was a quite hefty ten-pound three-ounce baby boy when he entered the world. His daddy Big Earl, no small man himself, exclaimed, "Hubba Bubba! That's a big boy you done pushed out there, Char-Donae."

The name stuck and Char-Donae decided she wasn't birthing any more babies. I would imagine a baby that big would cure almost any woman from wanting to have another one.

The fish camp was really a restaurant although I did know there were some moldy-smelling cabins that could be rented for those wanting to go bass fishing in the St. Johns River. The restaurant was a wooden structure stretching out over a marshy area with a dock guiding you into the restaurant. The décor was rustic for that more authentic feel of being close to the real natives of Northeast Florida.

I'll let you in on a little secret. It was a very carefully cultivated atmosphere. Hubba Bubba had gotten an interior design intern from the University of Florida to create the interior decor for her final class project. He also might have dated her during the design process. The rumor was she had done it for free.

The interior looked very old Florida but without the cheesiness that so many Florida waterfront restaurants have.

Old wooden plank flooring, numerous mounted fish, rods, reels, and used fishnets were hanging on the walls. It had a cluttered, homey feel while still letting in plenty of light so you knew what you were eating.

You could also sit outside on the deck and enjoy your fresh fried fish with your favourite adult liquid libation complete with watching boats ease their way up to the floating dock.

On Friday and Saturday nights you could listen to whatever music band Hubba Bubba had playing. Dancing wasn't only allowed but encouraged. Let's just say most of these folks aren't going to be on any TV dance shows any time soon.

Interrupting my thought process, Hubba Bubba semi-groused as he let loose with a very unsightly stream of brown juice over the railing, "Can you believe her, Parker? I swear she just flirts with everyone."

I couldn't help it, I laughed as little rivers of salty perspiration were coursing their way down my face and ruining what tiny bit of makeup I wore. "Are you serious? Miss Maisy is a pink flamingo and you're jealous of her?"

Wiping the sweat from my brow, we're way past the delicate euphemism of perspiration, this was full-out sweat running rivets from my hairline down to my chin. My hand swiping at my facial human body water had all the effects of a windshield wiper in a Florida summer rain downpour aka virtually nothing.

"You don't understand," Hubba Bubba spit his dip juice again off to the side, "I have people who are just coming to look at her...and they're not even staying to eat."

I was hoping my eyebrow sweat wouldn't seep down and temporarily blind me. "Why don't you charge for shrimp to throw out to her? Can you get Miss Maisy to pose in front of a Hubba Bubba's Fish Camp sign? She can stand in front of it."

He scratched the top of his curly red hair. "I dunno, Parker. The most I've ever been able to get her to do is to, maybe, wander over to me to eat some wet dog kibble out of a cup."

Slightly shaking my head and hoping my facial sweat wasn't going to hit him like a wet dog shaking itself off, I said, "There you go. Sell a souvenir cup, sell the dog kibble, and maybe charge for a picture with Miss Maisy."

He was still staring at the pink flamingo slowly moving around in the marshy water. I'll give him credit, he had put up a fence around her area to keep her safe from the gators. They would periodically show up at the fence and gaze longingly at what would be a very easy and tasty hors d'oeuvres if allowed to visit Miss Maisy.

"Parker, what made you come down to the fish camp? I thought you only hung out at The Capt'n's Table."

Turning toward the crushed coquina shell and Florida sand parking lot, I simply pointed. Heading toward us were the Lady Gatorettes – Misty Dawn, Myrtle Sue, Mary Jane, Flo, and Rhonda Jean.

Yes, many females in the South come from the womb with two names. A word to the wise, do not, repeat, do not make the error of referring to a two named woman with only one of her names. You will have committed the ultimate faux pas and the consequences aren't always pretty to the offending individual.

All five of the hormonally challenged, caffeine-and-sugar infused women I was happy to call my friends. Trust me when I say they're much better as friends and not as enemies. They could be scary on a good day and absolutely terrifying on a bad day.

Hubba Bubba had looked over his shoulder when I pointed and literally shuddered. Keep in mind, this hulking big man had played against some of the meanest and most ferocious football players ever in college football and in the NFL. To see him quiver...well, let's just say I thought it was funny, my shoulders started shaking, and I laughed. Out. Loud.

He glared at me for a moment, spit some more nasty salvia out, and stomped off for the safety and sanctity of his restaurant. He disappeared behind the wood doors.

The girls were dancing, bobbing, maybe twirling a little, and generally acting like complete goofballs strutting their stuff through the sandy parking lot. Decked out in cut-off jean shorts, not the Daisy Duke kind, Gator tee shirts, Gator hats tilted at various angles on their heads, orange and blue flip flops they were ready to chow down.

"Yo, yo, what up?" shouted Rhonda Jean as she put her finger on top of her head and spinning around in a circle.

Even though I was miserable with not a dry spot on my body due to the high humidity level, their exuberant behavior caused me to laugh. I hadn't seen them in a couple of days, every day was the norm, and I was glad we were getting together for a meal that wasn't coffee and doughnuts or pizza and Coke. Of course, fried fish, fried veggies, and French fries wasn't the healthiest of meals either, but it was far superior to our normal fare.

The smell of the hot fish oil cooking fried catfish permeated the air. It was discreetly masking the smell of the moldy river water lapping against the boat dock.

Misty Dawn, the ringleader, suddenly stopped and pointed at the flamingo slowly wading around in the marshy area just past the back deck of the restaurant. "What is that...that pink something doing out there?"

"Flamingo. It's a flamingo, Misty Dawn," explained Myrtle Sue wiping the sweat from her face. "Go stand up close to the fence and I'll take a picture of you."

Whipping her head around and dipping her head slightly, Misty Dawn gave a death stare to Myrtle Sue who promptly rolled her eyes saying, "All you had to do was say no. Whatever."

Before we go any further, I guess I should introduce myself and the Lady Gatorettes.

I'm Parker Bell, a boutique cyber security company owner and bestselling author of several books on true crime. Unfortunately, the true crime stories had happened right here in Po'thole, pronounced Poat – like goat, and hole.

Typically, it was called Pothole by anyone north of the Florida Georgia state line. The natives refer to this little hinky dinky town on the beautiful St. Johns River as Po Ho.

I'm surprised I'm not listed on the FBI's list of the Ten Most People Not To Hang Around If You Value Your Life list. Why? Because, cough, cough, all of the true crime stories...okay, let's just be honest and say, all of the murders happened in my vicinity. I did not commit any of these murders! Things just somehow magically seem to happen in my life.

Living in Atlanta for years, yes, I had escaped this godforsaken little backwoods town and moved to the big city, somehow I kept being lured back to Po Ho. A rubberband could only be stretched so far before it would either break or snatch you back. So far, it hadn't broken and I was always snatched back.

Finally realizing I was stuck in the twilight zone, I decided to move back to Po Ho. No one was more surprised than I to discover I actually had friends here. In Atlanta, I woke up one day and realized I didn't know a single soul I could call and go for coffee. Employees don't count.

As crazy and out of control as the Lady Gatorettes could be they were a lot of fun to be around. Even though this was a small town, and we knew almost everyone in it, we were all on a first name basis with local law enforcement due to the unfortunate murders that seemed to pop up around us on a fairly regular basis.

Let me be fair and say, I do have other friends here but after I had kept the girls, and specifically Misty Dawn, out of jail awhile back, I was their new BFF and they had voted me in as a member of the Lady Gatorettes.

What did this mean in the overall course of life? I was a little more likely to be let into a store or a restaurant without people cringing and trying to somewhat discreetly escape from being around the other girls. Apparently, I may have a calming effect on some of the townspeople.

Like Hubba Bubba trying to stay far, far away from the girls, the rest of the townspeople did pretty much the same thing. Since I hadn't jumped up on a table or thrown doughnuts at anyone or harmed anyone, I was safe...maybe.

Their over-the-top exuberance could be a wee bit unnerving for those who had never witnessed their display of unlimited energy.

Their version is they're very high energy. The rest of the world's version is they are beyond hyper, and sugar and caffeine are a legal drug they have no business consuming...ever.

Brazilian monkeys on a cotton candy sugar high were probably calmer than the girls when they got excited about something, which was pretty much anything.

Misty Dawn was still pointing at Miss Maisy when Rhonda Jean slapped her finger. "It's not nice to point, Misty Dawn."

Realizing World War III was about to descend upon anyone in the parking lot, I decided to step up and take one for the team. Yes, my little hamster started spinning like crazy on his tiny little wheel in my head. I do believe I heard him screaming, "Danger, Will Robinson, danger!" I ignored him.

"Whoa, whoa, whoa!" I stepped between Rhonda Jean and Misty Dawn stretching my arms to either side to keep them from coming any closer to each other. With me in the middle, I was pretty sure I would continue to live. "Ladies, we're going to have a nice dinner out on the deck, remember? Misty Dawn can tell us why she has such an aversion to Miss Maisy."

They were giving each other the stink eye while doing their version of two bulls facing each other and snorting. You know the look where you hope someone just shrivels up, turns into a prune, and dies.

My stink eye, on the other hand, has the effect of people thinking I'm squinting. They think one of my eyelashes has suddenly decided to escape from my eyelid and has dive-bombed into my orbital cavity. Meaning, of course, that my glare has absolutely no effect on anyone.

With any of the Lady Gatorettes, their stink eye would cause the devil to wither away into nothingness. Until you've had the non-pleasure of being laser-beamed with one of their evil, you're-gonna-die eyes you don't know the pain of feeling your life-supporting organs turn into mush. I don't wish that on anyone.

They had backed away from each other, still glaring. I was once again wiping the sweat from my brow and trying to keep the faint breeze from gluing my baby-fine, wet, brown hair to the front of my face and blinding me.

As we sat down at one of the tables on the deck, I could see out of the corner of my eye that the waitresses were having a healthy discussion, complete with arm raising and the oh-no-you-didn't snap, as to who was going to have the honor of waiting on us.

Finally, a gal came over. She had the weary look of life wasn't kind but was doing the best she could.

"Alright, y'all," she snapped her gum, "we've got ground rules for y'all since we know your reputation."

For most people, groans would have gone up but, no, these are the Lady Gatorettes and they take great pride in their off-the-wall reputation.

They all turned and high-fived each other with a couple of "Go Gators!" chants thrown in there.

The waitress rolled her eyes, turned and stared at the other waitresses still standing in a huddle. She may or may not have given them a three-finger salute.

"Listen up," she snapped, "y'all ain't having no food fights, jumping in the river, stealing a boat or jet ski, or getting in Miss Maisy's pond. Y'all darn sure better not be messing with Miss Maisy 'cas Hubba Bubba will throw you outta here." She glared at each of us. "Forever."

We looked at each other, grinned, and did the Gator Chomp.

She had her pen and pad ready. "I'm Jennie..."

"Jennie from the block," whooped the girls standing and doing their version of J Lo dancing. She has nothing to worry about.

Shaking her head, Jennie did a one eighty and left. She'd be back.

The girls continued to dance for a moment before plopping back down into the plastic chairs.

"I need a Coke." Mary Jane's face was looking, um, shall we say, very natural. Her makeup had completely slid off due to the Florida high heat and humidity.

If you're a girly-girl and plan on visiting Florida any time between the end of April and Thanksgiving, just know being outside for any length of time, that would be ten minutes, your makeup will never look or be the same ever again. You have been warned.

"Beer."

"Nope, I want a Coke." Mary Jane was firm. She turned around looking for Jennie. "Where is that girl?"

We started waving. Jennie broke from the waitress huddle and reluctantly came back. She looked defeated. "You ready to order?"

We did. Misty Dawn was staring at the pink flamingo slowly moving around in her little area.

"I know I've seen that bird somewhere else," she finally stated. "Where did Hubba Bubba get it?"

"It's a her," explained Flo, bobbing her head up and down to get Miss Maisy's attention. The flamingo wasn't paying any attention to anyone.

Misty Dawn was persistent. "Where did Hubba Bubba get her?"

I shrugged. Jennie was back and placing our drinks on the table.

"Jennie." That was not a question from Misty Dawn, it was a statement. "Tell Hubba Bubba I have a question for him."

She looked up as she was balancing her drink tray. "He might not be here."

"He's here. He was in the parking lot when we came in. I saw him."

"He scooted back into the restaurant." Hey, I was trying to be helpful. At least, I didn't say he was a big wimp when he saw the girls and had run for cover. It's called avoidance confrontation.

She nodded. "I'll get him."

The big man came out a few minutes later. He wasn't in any hurry to get to our table. He had plastered one of those big fake smiles on his face.

"Well, ladies, to what do I owe this pleasure? I thought y'all only hung out at The Capt'n's Table."

"Heard good things about you. Where didja get that flamingo?" Misty Dawn was direct. Subtlety did not reside in her DNA.

Never faltering, he smiled. "My girlfriend Trixie gave her to me."

"Is that Miss Trixie Delight from down at Babes, Babes, and More Babes?" Misty Dawn had a big cheesy grin on her face as she put down her Coke.

"Well, yes." Hubba Bubba was a little hesitant and having a hard time maintaining his composure. "Do you know Trixie?"

"Probably not as well as you do," smirked Misty Dawn taking a sip of her Coke. "Where did she get it?"

Shrugging and lifting his hands as he looked around at the other patrons sitting out on the deck before answering, "I don't know. I didn't ask. She said it was a gift for the restaurant. Why?"

"I'm pretty sure that bird is from that tourist trap down by Fort Lauderdale." Misty Dawn never took her eyes off him. "Are you sure you got it legally?"

Hubba Bubba was irate. Squaring up his shoulders, "Are you accusing my girlfriend of stealing a flamingo just to get my attention, Misty Dawn? I'll have you know..."

"Nope, not insinuating anything." She grinned and wiped the sweat from her face. "Just saying that bird might have another home."

"Flamingos pretty much all look the same," harrumphed Hubba Bubba, annoyed at the conversation and started to ease away from the table.

"That's like saying all dogs look the same. Not true, each animal is different. Just saying."

"Listen here, Misty Dawn, not that it's any of your business, but I have a completely legal bill of sale. Y'all are welcome to stay and enjoy your dinner or you can leave. Up to you."

Waving at Dr. Jeff Lumley and his wife Kim, he sauntered over to join them at their table for a moment before glaring at us once again before stomping back into the restaurant.

In all honesty, I couldn't blame him for being mad. The girls, and Misty Dawn in particular, had that effect on others. They played hard ball on asking questions.

As Mary Jane is fond of pointing out, "We ask questions others want to know but are afraid to ask."

I once tried alluding to that most of the time it's no one's business on those types of issues, especially ours. They ignore me and continue to ask those 'inquiring minds want to know' questions.

It's probably time for me to finish introducing you to everyone.

Misty Dawn, the leader of the Lady Gatorettes, would have made the perfect Navy Seal. Swift, silent, and deadly is her motto. She's tall, bronzed, straight dark brown hair, and looks like she could compete in the Olympics in any sport. She's definitely not as dainty as her name would imply.

At the time of her birth on a foggy morning, her mother, who may or may not have been heavily sedated at the time, declared to the doctor and nurse she saw an angel from God descending from the ceiling. The angel declared the name of the little precious girl child was to be Misty Dawn.

Let me just go on record saying Misty Dawn is anything but dainty. She is a strong leader. Attila the Hun would be proud of her.

She can outswear *any* military personnel. She has come up with swear word variations that has left me puzzled at times but knowing I have been chewed up and spit out by the best.

Apparently, I'm somewhat of a good influence on her because I've started noticing recently that she is substituting some of my clean swear words for her really offensive ones.

Yes, yes, we all *know* what I mean but I'm choosing to keep my swear words a wee bit more ladylike.

Pul-leaze, if you continue to laugh like that you may choke and die. I certainly don't want your death on my conscience.

Let me just say fudge nuggets and shish kebob are perfectly acceptable words to use in mixed company or around those inquisitive little creatures known as children. If they repeat my words, which they are prone to do, they are perfectly a okay to be used.

Misty Dawn's husband, John Boy, works in construction and is afraid of no one except his wife. If she so much as gives him a side stink-eye look, he turns into a major pile of mush and apologizes for everything and anything. It's not an attractive attribute for a husband.

Mary Jane is a very attractive brunette, has large brown puppy dog eyes, and is always surfing the internet for dates. She is a major flirt with any man she sees.

Once in a while, one of the girls will make a half-hearted attempt to remind, or scold her depending on your viewpoint, 'Mary Jane the internet isn't always safe for picking up men and dating them.' Mary Jane thinks they're jealous.

She's been known to stalk Joe D. Savannah, my first love boyfriend from waaay back in the day, on various dating websites. Her version is she's keeping track of him so she doesn't show up on his 'we might be a match' profile. Trust me, she won't.

Since Joe D. and I had had a serious relationship many years ago, Mary Jane considers it her sacred duty to inform me when he's single again. I do not care...which she simply cannot seem to understand.

She went to Atlanta shortly after her high school graduation for a fun-filled weekend with some out-of-town cousins. Keep in mind, this was more than a couple of years ago.

Speculation is she 'might' have indulged in some cheap illegal street pharmaceuticals that still show up periodically with her twitching at odd times and gibbering ridiculous sounding words that make absolutely no sense to anyone except her.

Those out-of-town cousins may be residing in a long-term stay-cation facility for leading others down the primrose path of sin. They've never come to see her again.

Myrtle Sue, short and close to the ground, is a domestic goddess. She knows every recipe that has ever been used on the Food Network channel.

She has a tiny volcano living inside of her although she's the epitome of calmness. Looks are deceiving.

Myrtle Sue's husband, J.W., apparently needed a reminder of her explosive temper a year or so ago.

Southern boys don't believe it's necessary to ask their wives for permission to go hunting or to explain why they go off in the woods with other men getting sweaty, stinky, dirty, nasty, and still don't have a dead animal to show for what they were doing over the weekend. They just grab their guns and go.

Myrtle Sue had come home from a particularly bad time at Wal-Mart only to discover J.W. had gone off for the weekend with the boys.

He did leave her a note. The really unfortunate part was he forgot to write "I love you" after requesting clean clothes for Monday.

Her hormones were already a wee bit on the explosive side since shopping at Walmart was never a happy experience for her. It was also that special time of the month.

Mount Vesuvius probably didn't explode like Myrtle Sue did. In a fit of anger, she took all of his clothes, threw them out in a heap on their driveway, poured deer musk oil on them, and proceeded to mix everything together like she would have for a Caesar salad. For those not in the know, deer musk oil has a sharp, repulsive ammonia and urine smell. She vowed she wasn't washing any more of J.W.'s clothes.

After becoming a graduate of the 90-day Myrtle Sue School of Doing Your Own Laundry, J.W. now leaves notes with a great big "I Love You" on them.

Myrtle Sue took this unhappy episode of her life, turned it into a book and is now a bestselling author on marital bliss with over fifty thousand copies sold. Yeah, I couldn't believe it either.

Rhonda Jean is the most, um, Rubenesque of the girls. As she so elegantly puts it, she's not p-h-a-t, she just has a few extra voluptuous curves that have decided to stay with her...permanently. She thinks her curves have an attitude. When it was suggested awhile back that she might want to consider joining a gym to firm up those jiggly curves, her comment was, "I'm just not highly motivated to do anything about it."

She is also the football trick play master. She knows every trick play that has ever been in a University of Florida Gator game for the past thirty-five years. She very firmly believes at least one trick play should be incorporated into every game...and sends both offensive and defensive coaches her super-secret trick playbook at the beginning of each season.

Her fervent wish is that one of her plays will be used during a televised game and the Gators will run it in for a touchdown. So far, the coaches have not used any of her plays.

Her husband, Big T, short for Thomas the Third, is very proud of his wife's initiative. He also engages in numerous outdoor activities that may or may not be legal involving gators, deer, bears, snakes, and any other exotic Florida creatures.

Flo is a tall, recently blonde out-of-the-bottle, former waitress who marries during off-season. This probably explains why she never notices her choice of men know nothing about Gator football. She and Mary Jane are always on the male patrol. We have to watch them like a hawk.

We all live in this delightful, not, little town of Po'thole, pronounced Po Ho by the locals and Pothole by anyone north of the Florida-Georgia state line. Technically, it's pronounced Poat, like goat, and Hole but rarely does anyone actually say the name right.

One would think as often as we make the national news that a television anchor would actually learn how to say the name of the town correctly.

Po Ho is located on the beautiful St. Johns River in northeast Florida.

Me? My motto should be "I see dead people" because murders and dead people seem to show up near me on a disturbingly regular basis.

Things have calmed down a bit right now with the girls, probably all of the fried catfish they were consuming with gusto. They were quiet. Well, sort of.

Restaurants should never run all-you-can-eat specials when the Lady Gatorettes are anywhere nearby. They could put most large men to shame with their copious consumption of food.

Seriously, I don't understand why these women don't weigh five hundred pounds or more. Their caloric intake was phenomenal. Me, on the other hand, if I ate an entire pizza by myself, I'd gain ten pounds.

The only thing I could think of was Misty Dawn must have them on some specialty Marine Corp exercise program and did not deem me worthy enough to be included.

That's okay with me, I don't like to exercise anyway. That alone seemed to excite my little hamster. His spinning merrily around to nowhere on his tiny little wheel was enough exercise for both of us.

Jennie came back around to pick up the empty platters. She looked a little dejected. "More?" Her eyes stared in disbelief with the I-can't-believe-you-ate-all-of-that look.

I leaned forward, wiggled my forefinger at her, and gave her the best news any server wants to hear. "Listen, I know this is a one price meal. I also know we've run you ragged on bringing all of this food over to us. I also know you didn't want to wait on us," I smiled while looking her in the eye, "because of our nasty reputation. However, you may not know that we tip very, very well."

I held up my hand as she started to make a feeble attempt to say something. "I also know that any time someone says they tip well that usually means they're awful tippers. We're not those people."

Motioning my finger for her to come closer to me, I mentioned a large dollar amount and that it would be in cash. She leaned back on her heels and smiled. Her face lit up. "Really?"

I nodded my head yes. "I'm the one paying the bill and that's what I think you deserve for today."

She smiled and headed back for the waitress huddle area. She may have bragging rights for the best tip of the day. I don't know if waitresses compare tips or not.

"How much did you have to pay to keep her bringing more food?" Mary Jane popped another little round hushpuppy in her mouth.

"Aarrgghh!" shouted Misty Dawn jumping up from the table and pointing. "That, that pink thing keeps staring at me. I want it to go away!"

"I think you've got mother issues," snorted Myrtle Sue, looking up from her coleslaw and fried catfish. "You might want to talk to a therapist about that."

Flo was twirling her fork in the grits, God had a bad day when He made that. "Is it that time of the month for you, Misty Dawn? Miss Maisy..."

It suddenly occurred to me Misty Dawn had never explained her aversion to the flamingo when we were talking earlier. She might have an interesting elucidation.

Misty Dawn glared at all of them, looked at Miss Maisy who was slowly making her way over to the deck railing. There was a bar about two feet in front of the railing keeping Miss Maisy and the customers from becoming BFFs.

"Y'all can find your own way home!" She threw down her napkin, grabbed her Coke, and torpedoed her way out to her truck in the parking lot.

Rhonda Jean laughed as she licked her fingers, "So glad we all came in our own vehicles." Turning to the other girls, "What's up with her?"

Everyone shrugged and went back to eating catfish. Looking back on things, one of us should have probably gone after Misty Dawn and tried to find out what was going on with her. Hindsight is always twenty-twenty.

CHAPTER 2

I told you Miss Maisy was lonesome," snapped Trixie as she sashayed her way across the deck with Hubba Bubba following along behind her. He was watching one of her more voluptuous assets and promptly ran into her when she suddenly stopped.

"Hubba Bubba, would you please pay more attention and stop running into the back of me." She half turned to him, frowned, and then pointed in the direction of three men escorting three more flamingos to Miss Maisy's pond.

"Why are they using a U-Haul truck?" asked Hubba Bubba. At least now he was looking up from his formerly downward attraction to Trixie's bottom half.

The pink birds were making their way out of the truck and gently high stepping into the marshy water. They were speaking the language of their people – nasal honking, growling, and low gabbing.

They were also very aware of having an audience of very attentive diners and decided they'd start behaving like the stars they knew they were. Preening this way and that, they slowly made their way into the pond.

"You know more than two flamingos are called a flamboyance, don't you?" shouted Flo to Hubba Bubba and Trixie who were ignoring her. She was now looking around for Jennie to bring some more fried catfish. I think this was round number seven on the food. I quit counting after three times.

I didn't know what a group of flamingos were called but I sure wasn't going to admit that one of the Lady Gatorettes might have a vital need-to-know piece of information that was not swimming around in my head just waiting to come out.

We watched as Hubba Bubba just stared at the three newest members of his pink harem daintily edging their way over to introduce themselves to Miss Maisy.

Like a queen waiting on her servants, she almost bid them to come closer. She nodded her head royally acknowledging their presence into her sanctuary.

"See, Hubba Bubba, I knew they would all get along well with each other." Trixie was happy with a big smile as she threw her arms around him. Well, as much as she could. He was a big, tall man.

He bent over and laid his head on top of her heavily sprayed hair. I'm surprised his face didn't bounce back but I'm guessing he's practiced this move once or twice before.

Trixie is the star performer at the Babes, Babes, and More Babes gentlemen's club...or at least that's what I've been told. I've personally never been in the joint.

Her stage name is Miss Trixie Delight. Yeah, it's a real stretch for her stage name and her alleged personal name to be so far apart. I strongly suspect that's not her real name and I would hazard a not nice thought she's probably seen the inside of a jail cell on more than one occasion.

Rhonda Jean nodded at Trixie and sort of whispered, not really, but at least it wasn't at her normal volume, "Big T says she can dance real good."

Mary Jane, Flo, and I all cut sideway glances at each other. Kind of surprised Rhonda Jean let Big T go to a strip, er, my bad, gentlemen's, club and I was even more surprised that she would say that out loud.

Myrtle Sue started to giggle. "J.W. says she bounces in all of the right places."

"That's what good plastic surgery will do for you," laughed Flo, lightly tapping her chest above her breasts.

We all snickered some more.

Inquiring minds had to ask. "Um, how do you...?

"Let the boys go to Babes?" finished Rhonda Jean. Jennie had finally stopped bringing us individual plates and replaced it with one big platter of heaping, hot fried catfish and numerous little hushpuppies on the side. Rhonda Jean took two big filets before continuing. "John Boy, J.W., and Big T all go once a month. They get drunk, spend some money, feel like manly men, come home, and pass out in bed."

Myrtle Sue smirked, grabbing another fried catfish filet. "Gets them out of our hair for a while."

"Should we tell them?" winked Rhonda Jean as she so daintily picked up a whole filet and bit the end off.

Flo, Mary Jane, and I looked questioningly at them. Finally, because I have the patience and attention span of a gnat, I said, "Okay, I'll bite. What do y'all do when the guys are out having fun? I'm guessing Misty Dawn is also with you."

"What?!" screeched Flo. She almost jumped to her feet. She was incensed. "Y'all are doing something without ALL OF US? That's, that's, that's..."

"Unamerican," snapped Mary Jane as she broke her whole fried catfish in half. She was upset.

Me? I was more curious than anything else. I continued to eat what was on my plate. From round one. I wasn't even on my second helping of anything.

"Calm down," laughed Rhonda Jean picking up some more hushpuppies. "Y'all aren't invited because you don't have husbands and..."

"I've been married," harrumphed Flo not being pacified.

"Your husbands are not like our husbands." Rhonda Jean was trying to explain.

"Mine are not rednecks," sniffed Flo. I noticed she had turned her plastic spork upside down and gripped the handle perhaps a tad too tightly. Was she making this plastic, easily breakable eating utensil a weapon? If so, she should probably choose something more substantial.

I had also observed by glancing around at different tables, other diners had real flatware not the plastic kind we were given. I guess

Hubba Bubba must have anticipated the possibility of a free-for-all once we entered his restaurant and decided to limit the amount of damage the Lady Gatorettes could inflict.

Thankfully, Rhonda Jean ignored her comment. "We take turns going to each other's house."

And for the piece de'resistance, Myrtle Sue announced, "We watch Magic Mike."

"Aarrgghh!" Flo groaned and faked a swooning posture by falling flat on the tabletop.

You could see red flames shooting from Mary Jane's eyes. "You didn't think we would want to watch that movie with you?" Her words were clipped, her tone was low, and I scooted back in my chair. Hey, I value my life. Plus, I may or may not be a coward in certain circumstances.

Mary Jane, never looking in my direction, uttered the words that usually caused my heart to drop down to my toes. "What do you think about this, Parker?"

I was the de facto leader when Misty Dawn wasn't around. I could easily run a multi-million-dollar cyber security company with an iron fist and incredible focus but, eh, not so much with these girls.

"I think it doesn't make one wit of difference if they watch Magic Mike once a month or not. Since we do so much together, sometimes it's just nice to have a break." I was gathering up steam. "Why don't you and Flo have your own movie night?"

Surprisingly, that thought had never entered anyone's mind because they seemed to be deliberating on what I had suggested.

Finally, Flo, semi-grinning, gave me a wink. "So, Parker, you can come to my house on Tuesday with Mary Jane and we'll have our own party."

"Nope, unt uh."

I was surprised at Mary Jane's swift reaction. So was Flo who immediately demanded, "Why not?"

"You live out in the middle of nowhere in that trashy mobile home and I'm not doing it. Y'all can come to my house."

Frowning for just a moment, Flo acquiesced with a big smile on her face. "Okay, but you do remember that trashy mobile home out front is just for show, right? You've been to my very nice house before."

"Oh, yeah, I forgot but I'm still not going out that far. Plus, you've got that Casper snake guarding your house."

I couldn't help it, I laughed. Flo did have a large albino rat snake guarding the hidden door to her house. He was a little unnerving because he liked to come out of his hide-y hole and introduce himself with what I'm sure he thought was a seductive grin. For those of us who are not overly fond of those long wiggly things on the ground, there was absolutely nothing remotely tantalizing about his smile.

Flo's trashy mobile home was a decoy to keep any potential new husbands from thinking she had any money.

All of the Lady Gatorettes were doing very well financially. They had made out like bandits on cashing in on their reality tv and national radio shows. Plus, all of their speaking engagements and personal appearances brought in a substantial amount as well.

They were now trying to be somewhat low-key because each one had decided the national scrutiny of their private lives was just too much.

While they lived on social media and loved their adoring fans, they did not take kindly to hater remarks and often unleashed on those folks before deleting them from their feed.

At one point, it had turned into a badge of honor to be kicked off a Lady Gatorette social media platform. The girls had finally hired a social media company to handle everything for them.

For a while, the chances of anyone actually connecting or communicating with the girls was between slim to none and Slim went to the Bahamas.

Finally deciding they could handle the limelight again but on their own terms, the girls decided to only post a couple of times a week. The first five or six people who actually responded to a post would get a comment or thumbs up from them but after that they didn't engage with their fans.

Since Flo had this relatively new cute blond out-of-a-bottle hairdo, she had a lot of male followers who often posted their undying love for her and umpteen marriage proposals. Unfortunately, many of those proposals came from long-term stay-cation residents.

It appeared my suggestion on having Flo, Mary Jane, and myself having our own movie night quieted everything down.

I was silently congratulating myself when my hamster started bouncing up and down on his tiny little wheel.

Just why do I get these weird thoughts at the most inopportune times?

CHAPTER 3

Hubba Bubba continued to stare at the new flamingos while Trixie waved at the men in the U-Haul truck.

Flo grinned at us. Oh, no. I wasn't sure what was going to happen, but I suspected it wasn't going to be good.

"Hubba Bubba," she gleefully shouted, almost jumping up and down, "do we get to name the birds?"

Trixie whipped around faster than any spin she probably did on a dancer's pole. Pointing a finger at our table, she snarled, "This has nothing to do with you. Eat your catfish."

Whoa! She certainly wasn't going to be voted for Miss Congeniality by our group and, from the looks of other diners, not by them either. Hubba Bubba was well-liked. And Trixie? Well, not so much, and especially not by a lot of women.

Hubba Bubba turned around and put on the congenial host's smile. "No. Their names are Miss Pinkie, Miss Lexie, and Miss Diamond."

As he went to put his arm around Trixie, she slapped his hand. "THOSE are NOT the names they're going to be called! I've already chosen their names."

Hubba Bubba looked a little confused, a lot embarrassed, and not happy. "Trixie, you just said you gave them to me. Therefore, I can call them whatever I want. Those are my favorite dancers."

Trixie exploded on him screaming, "I am your favorite dancer! How dare you, how dare you have any other ones! You can just sleep by yourself tonight!" She was screaming obscenities as she wiggled her way across the deck and heading out to the U-Haul.

Mary Jane twitched and before any of us could stop her she had thrown her empty Coke can at Trixie and hit her in the back of her shellacked hairdo.

Screaming and turning around, Trixie looked at our table. We simply sat there with food halfway to our mouths. Mary Jane stood up. "You shut your trashy mouth right now, Trixie. There are families here with kids and you should know better than to say those words in front of kids."

Trixie bounced over to Mary Jane, she stood a good three or four inches taller than Mary Jane and pointed her finger at her.

All of us scooted our chairs back a little. I'm not going to lie, I was a wee bit concerned there was going to be a free for all and I'd have to call Missy, my assistant in Atlanta, to get us out of jail.

Mary Jane took a step forward into Trixie's space, never let it be said that a Lady Gatorette would back down from a confrontation, and warned, "You so much as touch me..."

Trixie squinched her face up, growled, and leaned forward, "Or what, you little pique squeak?"

Mary Jane never blinked her eyes. She never clinched her fists. She never said another word. She kept staring into Trixie's eyes.

Trixie's false eyelashes started rapidly opening and closing after five seconds. Taking a deep breath, she took a half step back, turned on her stiletto high heels, and bounced off the deck.

Let me just go on record saying performers are a wee bit on the dramatic side.

Grinning, Mary Jane sat back down to her fried catfish. "That's how you do it."

Intimidation at its finest. I'd seen Misty Dawn do that before but never one of the other girls.

A man from the next table over leaned back in his chair and waved at Mary Jane. "Hey, thanks for doing that."

She smiled and nodded. "Trixie's got no business saying them ugly words in front of kids."

A couple of other families came over and thanked her as they were leaving. Who knew the Lady Gatorettes could have a positive influence on families and small children?

Hubba Bubba came over to our table, a little embarrassed. "Thanks, Mary Jane. I've never seen her back down before."

"That's cause you're a guy. She doesn't know what to do with a female who doesn't scream back at her and have threatening body language."

We all laughed. Flo smiled sweetly. "So, Hubba Bubba, you going to keep those names for your new pink ladies?"

He nodded, then smiled. "Y'all enjoy your catfish."

Sigh, if life were only that easy.

CHAPTER 4

After leaving the girls, the rest of my evening was quiet and enjoyable at home. The next morning, however, was not.

Dimwit aka Dewitt Munster, I kid you not his mother actually named him that, showed up at my door. His mother probably never even thought about nasty nicknames her Barney Fife look-alike, less than brilliant son would be called when he grew up.

Waving for Dimwit to come in, I was ever the gracious hostess. "There's coffee in the pot if you want some."

"I'm here on official business, Parker." He hitched up his green uniform pants that were hanging low on his hips. "Where were you last night?"

I furrowed my eyebrows together, jutted my chin out, and tapped my forefinger on my chin. "Um, why don't you tell me where I was?"

He was flustered. "I'm the one asking the questions, Parker, not you."

I took another sip of coffee. "You're in my house, Dewitt. What do you want?"

"Miss Trixie Delight is dead and you were the last person to see her alive."

I semi-shook my head and rolled my eyes. I picked up my coffee mug. "Are you serious? The last time I saw her was at Hubba Bubba's around five or so. She bounced out the door after spewing some ugly words at him. That's it. Never saw her again. Besides, which, what would be my motive?"

I drank some more coffee while he pondered what I said. As I mentioned, Dimwit wasn't the brightest bulb in the box. He had been elected sheriff by the slimmest of margins. A convicted drug dealer had lost to him by only five votes, that should tell you something about the confidence level the fine citizens of River County had for our illustrious sheriff.

He sputtered for a moment, "You gals don't have to have a reason to have murdered bodies show up near you."

Well, he kinda did have a point. Murders did seem to show up fairly frequently around me and the Lady Gatorettes. Things happen, people. We do not murder anyone.

"Dewitt, I have work to do," I stood up, hoping he would get the hint to leave. "Do you have a point here? How did Trixie die?"

"I take mine black."

"Excuse me." I was shocked. I really couldn't believe he was asking me to get him coffee in my house.

"Parker, I said I take my coffee black."

I saw red. Not the pretty red, I saw blood red and my little hamster was alternatively bouncing up and down on his little wheel and spinning it like crazy.

"OUT!" I roared pointing at the door. "Get out you incompetent idiot!"

"Who you calling incompetent, Parker?" He did start easing toward the door though.

"Get OUT, Dewitt! Don't you EVER come back on my property!" I advanced toward him.

My threatening posture and the evil look in my eye was enough to convince this poor excuse of a man he should exit my house pronto.

Except Dewitt didn't have the sense God gave a goose. He turned at the door, totally bug-eyed, and bouncing on his toes, and shouted, "Next time I'll be back with an arrest warrant!"

I threw my coffee cup at him. Unfortunately, my aim wasn't all that great and it whizzed past his head through the door's open space and landed in the yard. I was shocked I hadn't actually hit him and he had the Bambi-in-the-headlights look and skedaddled out the door letting it slam behind him.

Hearing a dog growl outside, I saw Potus, my illustrious German Shepherd who now lives with my former head of security Denny Rowe, had grabbed Dewitt's pants leg and proceeded to yank them down. This caused Dewitt's pants to drop to his ankles showing me his boxers decorated with...little candy hearts. I started to laugh.

Dewitt was screaming some very not nice things at my dog. Denny was laughing. He whistled and Potus immediately stopped. Potus had that satisfied tongue hanging out of his mouth smile as he bounced up to me.

Dewitt? Well, he yanked up his pants, still spewing obscenities, and left tire skid marks in my driveway.

Denny came in laughing and headed right for the coffee pot. Holding up a mug, he grinned. I nodded for a cup of the delicious brew of the gods.

Denny was ex-military. In fact, he was ex-special ops, had worked with me off and on for years, and we were not romantically involved although we bickered like an old married couple.

He was about six feet tall and somewhere in the neighborhood of two hundred pounds of pure muscle with lightning-fast responses. He was someone you wanted on your side in dicey situations.

Although he was a very attractive man with a great tan, dark brown hair, and brown eyes he simply had never made my heart go pitty-pat. Yes, I often wonder what is wrong with me. He'd be a great catch for any woman except he was not interested in marriage or any long-term relationships. He preferred his freedom as he was fond of telling girls on the first date. He didn't want to get their hopes up was his explanation.

"So, what do I owe this pleasure?"

Denny grinned. "What set you off on Dimwit?"

I shrugged, rolled my head back and forth, and took a sip of coffee. "Do I really need a reason?"

His eyebrows raised as he put the mug to his lips. "He insulted you in some form or fashion."

It wasn't a question.

I sighed. Might as well tell him the truth. "He marched in here, said Trixie Delight was dead, where was I last night, and oh, yeah," I snapped my fingers. "He wanted his coffee black."

Denny spewed coffee out of his mouth he was laughing so hard. He walked over to the counter, pulled a couple sheets of paper towels off the roll, and proceeded to mop up the coffee on the floor. "He asked you..."

I snorted. I had both hands on my hips. "He didn't ask, he TOLD me."

"Oh, that is beyond funny, Parker."

"Come on, Denny! Do I look like a flipping secretary to you?" I was starting to get steamed when I accidently sloshed some of my coffee on my laptop computer's keyboard. "Nooooo!" I semi-screamed as I turned to grab some paper towels.

Denny was bent over double laughing. Potus was wearing that big silly grin German Shepherds are known for. I hated them both at that moment.

My laptop hissed and the screen went black. "Noooo, noooo, noooo," I moaned turning the computer upside down and trying to shake the coffee out of it. "Noooo, noooo, noooo. Not now, not now."

I felt a major headache coming on. Denny had big water puddles rolling south on his face. I seriously hated him.

He finally managed to sputter out, "Should I call Missy and have her send you a new one?"

Was I never going to live down the curse of the laptops? Somewhere, maybe in a former life, I must have greatly angered the computer gods because on a regular basis...cough, cough...I somehow managed to spill liquids on my laptop and it would die an unnatural death, usually at the most inopportune time. I hated having to call my assistant Missy in Atlanta to overnight me a new one.

Biting the bullet, I called. She was very chirpy on answering.

"Parker, how's things in Po Ho?"

"Um, Missy, I, um..."

Yes, she started laughing. "Okay, a new laptop. Did coffee seep its way into the motherboard or did it take the scenic route of watching a cascading coffee fall and thus drowning the entire laptop?"

I hated her also. So far my day of hating people was growing.

"Missy," I growled.

"Oh, stop, Parker." She was still giggling. "Let Rhonda Jean know you need another computer. Before you ask, I sent her one last week."

"Really?" My little ears picked up. I'd have to rethink my hating her.

"Yes, because," she started to giggle again, "it's been almost a month since you ruined one and I thought it would be wise to have one locally for you."

"Well, wait a second," I was thinking it through. "Why send it to Rhonda Jean and not to me here at the house?"

"Do you really want to know the answer to that, Parker?"

Well, yeah, I kinda did. Her sending it to Rhonda Jean didn't make any sense to me.

"Because if I sent it to your house, you would know that it's there and you would be even less careful in taking care of it."

I shouldn't have asked. Unfortunately, she was probably right.

"Parker, once you get it, log into our portal, and we'll download everything you need."

"Um, thanks." Yes, I said it begrudgingly.

"Your gratitude is overwhelming," laughed Missy. "The good news is you won't need to wait until tomorrow to get it."

"Yeah, yeah, yeah. Later." I disconnected the call.

Denny was still laughing. "Missy sent it to Rhonda Jean?"

I just nodded. Words weren't necessary. Was I embarrassed? Not really, I just couldn't figure out why liquid kept finding its way to my computer because I did try really hard not to spill or have any type of fluid near the computer. Honestly, I do. However, since I'm a coffee addict, I do feel compelled to always have a cup of coffee within reach.

Thus, the unfortunate marriage of coffee with the laptop continued. This was not an unrequited love. They seemed to get together at every possible opportunity regardless of how hard I tried to keep them separated.

I texted Rhonda Jean to bring over my new laptop at her earliest convenience. Meanwhile, Denny had finally stopped laughing. Potus was licking up the coffee that had dripped off the table and onto the floor.

"Did you say Trixie Delight was dead?" He handed me a fresh cup of coffee. Okay, he was getting back into my good graces.

"Yes." I nodded as I took a sip of the very hot nectar of the gods. "Dimwit wanted to know where I was last night."

Looking out to the beautiful St. Johns River, I pondered what Trixie's death would mean. Snapping out of my thoughts, I said, "The girls and I went to Hubba Bubba's and..."

"Your new hangout or did you get thrown out of The Capt'n's Table?"

Shaking my head, "We had heard Hubba Bubba's food had greatly improved and it had been awhile since we'd been there so we thought we'd try it out.

"Did you know he's got Miss Maisy some new flamingo playmates?"

Denny wrinkled his brow, puzzled. "That's weird."

"What?"

"I thought Trixie didn't want him having any more flamingos." He looked at me conspiratorially. "What she wanted, she got."

I laughed. "What did she have on Hubba Bubba that he just rolled over and gave her anything she wanted?"

"Seriously, Parker? You have to ask a dumb question like that?"

Well, it was a dumb question on my part, but I didn't want to own up to it. "Besides the obvious man woman thing?"

"Parker, this explains why you're still single. Men only want a couple of things in life and..."

I put my hands over my ears. "Nope, don't want to hear it. You can blah, blah, blah all you want but say no more."

Rhonda Jean burst through my kitchen door with all the speed of a Gator defensive linebacker going for the quarterback. She slid to a stop nearly at my toes. "Here's your laptop, Parker. You've gone almost an entire month before killing another one. Is this a new record for you or what?"

I had better sense to say anything other than "Thank you, Rhonda Jean."

She went over to the counter and removed the empty pot. "No coffee? Parker, girl, what's wrong with you?"

Ignoring her again, I thought I'd find out if she knew anything about Trixie's death.

"Um, did you hear that Miss Trixie Delight is dead?"

She looked up from filling the pot with water. "Doesn't surprise me one bit. Lotta women, wives, didn't like her much. What happened?"

"Dimwit didn't tell me and he kinda left in a hurry."

She nodded sagely. "Yep, I saw his tire tracks out in the driveway."

She leaned down and scratched Potus' head. "You musta scared him, hummm, boy? Good boy."

That silly dog's tail thumped the floor. He did this with everyone but me.

"Yep, he pulled Dimwit's pants down enough to see that he had little candy hearts on his boxers." Denny wiggled one of his eyebrows.

As we were laughing, the rest of the Lady Gatorettes trouped through the door bearing gifts of doughnuts.

Mary Jane grabbed some paper plates and paper towels from the cabinet and tossed them out on the countertop. I guess she wasn't in her Martha Stewart hostess mode today.

She frowned at me.

Rut row. It was never a good sign when a Lady Gatorette did that.

"Thanks, Mary Jane." I smiled. "What's new?"

"Trixie's dead."

So much for small talk. "Yep, I heard that from Dimwit this morning. Y'all know any details?"

They all chimed in with "Yeah, he came to my house too," "Who does that idiot think he is to come to my house before 8?!" "None of us had anything to do with that."

Yeah, well, I knew that. None of us had any reason to get rid of Trixie. Plus, had any of us, me included, decided to get rid of someone, I can safely assure you that individual would never ever be found. We would all have airtight alibis.

I clapped my hands, "Ladies! Do we know where she was found or any other details?"

Misty Dawn cleared her throat, yeah, that's so ladylike. "As of ten minutes ago," she looked at her watch, "Dimwit arrested Hubba Bubba for her murder."

CHAPTER 5

K nock me over with a feather. We were all surprised. Hubba Bubba worshipped the ground Miss Trixie Delight walked on. There was no way he would have murdered her. I could, however, see her murdering someone.

"Ooo," squealed Myrtle Sue reaching for Misty Dawn's arm, "how did you get the police scanner on your watch?"

Misty Dawn grinned, held up her arm, and proudly marched around the kitchen turning her arm so all could admire her new watch.

"Parker's company sent me a prototype."

My eyes almost bugged out of my head. "Say what? I didn't know anything about this." My eyes narrowed. "Did you have my company create something for you?"

Her smile widened, looking much like the Cheshire cat in Alice in Wonderland. "Nope, JoJo in new product development offered it to me to try out."

I didn't even know who JoJo was but he, or she, was so fired.

"Out! Every one of you out on the pool deck right now." I was livid. How dare an employee of my company give something to someone else without running it through the proper channels.

"Um, Parker..."

"You too, Rhonda Jean. I'll talk to y'all in a few minutes." I was waiting on my ever-efficient assistant Missy to answer the phone.

"Hey, Parker, what's..."

"Who's JoJo?" I demanded. My eyes turned to the coffee pot, there was still some in brown juice in it.

"He's in product development." She paused, "I'm guessing Misty Dawn was showing off or demonstrating her new watch with the police scanner capability?"

I growled as I poured the last bit of coffee into my cup. "How did I not know about this? JoJo is so fired. Do it today."

Starting to disconnect, I heard her say, "Wait, wait, Parker. It's not what you think. Let me explain."

Looking at the phone for a moment, I punched the speaker button. "Yeah?"

"Rhonda Jean came up with the idea and actually sent us the schematics on how she thought it would work. She didn't know how to actually create the software to do that."

Taking a deep breath, "Surprisingly, her methodology was perfect. We created the software. JoJo called Misty Dawn to see if she would test it before we told you about it."

"Why?" I still wasn't happy about this breach of protocol.

"Because the girls are going to patent it." Missy's voice was soft. "They're going to give it to you as a birthday present. They believe it's going to make millions of dollars."

I was almost overcome with emotion. The Lady Gatorettes were going to give me a patent potentially worth millions of dollars.

"I'm, I'm speechless." Taking a deep breath, "Am I supposed to know that part?"

"Probably not."

"Are we going to have a conflict of interest on this product with our areas of security for the government? I can't imagine law enforcement is going to be very happy with us when it's released to the general public."

Missy started to laugh, "Well, the girls think it needs to be sold to the Mafia through an established bona fide company and let them handle the distribution and everything that goes along with that."

Shaking my head, the girls were smart. Honestly, that wasn't a bad idea. It kept all of us out of the doghouse with the government and my company could continue creating all of the nefarious software the general public would be appalled to know existed.

"Do you still want me to fire JoJo?"

"Naa, how soon do you think that would be ready to go to market?"

"The patent takes about two years, but we can start the manufacturing and sales process and add the words patent pending."

"Let me talk to the girls and I'll call you back. Have our patent attorney on standby."

Starting another pot of coffee, I waved for the girls to come back in.

John Wayne, or maybe it was Winston Churchill, who famously said, "Never apologize, never explain."

I'm not prone to apologizing.

Nodding towards the pot, "Fresh coffee."

They were silent, eyeing me warily.

"Rhonda Jean," I swear I thought I almost saw her cringe slightly, "how did you ever come up with the technology to have a police scanner on a watch? That's absolutely amazing."

The girls started grinning and high fiving each other followed by the Gator Chomp.

Rhonda Jean beamed. "Remember the old Dick Tracy watches? I just took the idea from there. I know you can find an app that does it but who wants to look at their phone all the time when it's just so much easier to look at your wrist. Plus," smiling wickedly, "if someone doesn't want you to know that you're looking at a scanner, they'll think you're just old-fashioned and looking at a watch."

Yes, there's a certain genius in that.

"Missy told me that y'all want to get a patent and give it to me." I had a questioningly look on my face.

They all nodded and smiled.

"Not going to happen…"

Misty Dawn snarled, "It's ours and we can do what we want."

Shaking my head, "Nope, we're going to set up another company with all of us and we all share in the profits."

Mary Jane wailed as she set her coffee mug down. "But it's our birthday gift to you. You've made us all millionaires what with the radio and tv shows and..."

"I appreciate your thoughts but y'all made me a Lady Gatorette and that's an honor I don't take lightly."

Misty Dawn clapped her hands. "Stop! Y'all are focusing on the wrong thing. We need to go get Hubba Bubba out of jail."

I held up my hand, hoping that maybe I outranked her in my own house although that might have been debatable. "Whoever came up with the idea of selling the watch to a legit Mafia business was brilliant. Okay, let's go visit Hubba Bubba."

We probably looked like the redneck version of the FBI pulling up to the sheriff's department. While they drove black SUVs for the most part, we showed up in our black trucks with the rollover cab bar complete with power actuated lights. If that didn't scream "Don't mess with us," the girls jumping down from the truck cab would certainly erase whatever notion someone might have about any of us being weak females.

Misty Dawn actually came with us as well even though Dimwit still thought she was responsible for several murders. Let me point out she had been cleared by the FBI, the government, all law enforcement with the exception of Dimwit.

She had it on good authority, a secretary in his office had told her, Dewitt wasn't in the building or even on the grounds. She was safe to come in without running into him.

I approached the bullet-proof plexiglass partition separating the administrative personnel from the less-than-desirable public.

Recognizing Lucy Lu from a previous unfortunate encounter when I inadvertently grabbed her and caused the buttons on her shirt to explode and roll everywhere.

She was left standing there, totally uncovered. Well, she did have on a Victoria's Secret bra and, I must admit, she filled hers out far better than I did mine.

I hoped she wouldn't remember me, but chances were high that she would. She did.

She eased out from behind her desk. Her body language was not one of happiness in seeing me.

"Parker." Her voice was flat.

"Hi, Lucy Lu. I didn't know you were working here now." I smiled hoping for some sense of camaraderie. My charming personality was not working on her.

"What do you want?"

Misty Dawn pushed me out of the way. "I see you're still going for Miss Congeniality, Lucy Lu. We need to see Hubba Bubba. What do we need to sign?"

Lucy Lu glared at Misty Dawn no doubt evaluating the strength of the plexiglass partition against a Lady Gatorette. She heartily exhaled air through her nose. "Let me see if he can have visitors."

Misty Dawn placed both hands on the counter and leaned forward until her nose almost touched the safety partition. "Don't you make me wait for more than five minutes."

Lucy Lu nodded, turned back to her desk and picked up the phone. The other girls in the administrative pool grinned and acknowledged Misty Dawn with a slight nod of their heads. Yep, safe to say, Lucy Lu wasn't one of their favorite people either.

"He's in holding at the moment but they're going to move him to the visitation room. Y'all going to have to empty your pockets before you can go in there."

"Give us the little plastic bins."

The girls were already pulling stuff out of their pockets. I strongly suspected they could turn their jeans into lethal weapons if the need ever arose. They had more snaps and zippers on their jeans than I did. I should probably ask the girls about getting some of those jeans.

Entering the visitation room which had all of the charm and warmth of a concrete bunker, everything was gray...the walls, the table, the metal folding chairs, everything.

The guard brought in Hubba Bubba, still handcuffed, and pushed him into a metal folding chair. He pointed at the camera in the ceiling and then at the picture glass window. "We can see and hear everything."

Before I could say anything, Misty Dawn snapped, "Which you cannot use in a court of law."

He shrugged and walked out of the room. The door clicked shut.

"Is that true, Misty Dawn?"

She raised her shoulders and let them fall. "I don't know but I'm betting he doesn't either."

I noticed she had pushed the Levi button at the top of her jeans. I kind of frowned, wondering what she was doing.

Flo popped up with, "They can see us, but their sound is going to come and go."

And that's the reason why I need to get some jeans like theirs. They have secret stuff in their jeans.

Hubba Bubba looked miserable. His head had been down when he first entered the room, he looked up with tears in his eyes. "I didn't do it. I swear I didn't do it. I loved Trixie."

Flo snickered. "You fall in love all the time, Hubba Bubba. What made you think you were in love with her?"

He looked up again, eyes still moist. "I know most people don't understand the entertainment industry..."

"Particularly for gentlemen who enjoy professional dancers." Mary Jane was grinning and wiggling her eyebrows.

Hubba Bubba ignored her. "Trixie had a bad childhood."

Myrtle Sue rubbed her first finger and thumb together. "That's the world's smallest record player playing my hearts bleeds for you."

He glared at her for a moment. "Anyway, she was going to stop dancing. She had offers all over the country."

"And that's the reason why she was dancing in this thriving metropolis of Po Ho." Yes, Rhonda Jean was being sarcastic. She sat down in one of the empty metal folding chairs.

Hubba Bubba grimaced, rubbing his cuffed hands through his hair. "Would you just let me finish?"

I rolled my first two fingers for him to hurry up and continue.

"Anyway, she thought we could make the fish camp a tourist destination with the flamingos. I had only wanted the one, Miss

Maisy, but Trixie wanted more. I didn't know she had ordered more until they showed up the other day when y'all were there.

"But since they showed up, I decided to name them and, as y'all saw, she wasn't real happy about me naming them."

Flo interrupted him, looking at the plate glass window. "What was she going to name them? Like Trixie one, Trixie two, Trixie three?"

I giggled. Hubba Bubba apparently didn't find the humor in that.

"Trixie had a real entrepreneurial spirit."

"I'll bet." I couldn't help myself, those words flew out of my mouth before I could stop them.

He slammed his hands down on the table. "Why did y'all come here if you weren't going to be helpful?" He looked around for the guard. Not seeing any help, he took a deep breath and exhaled it slowly. "I already have a website and we were going to start selling various products and we were going to have Miss Maisy as our spokesperson, our logo."

"Hubba Bubba, where and how did the sheriff's department find Trixie and how did they tie you to her murder?" Inquiring minds needed to know to be able to help him.

He looked a little sheepish. "Well, we mighta had an argument last night at the restaurant."

"About?" I was wondering how long we had before the Po Ho version of the Keystone Cops came back.

"The names of the flamingos."

Ah, a woman's jealousy over the names of pink birds. Unbelievable.

"Anyway, Trixie was unhappy and said she wouldn't be spending the night at my house and left. I went home and went to sleep. Next thing I knew Dewitt was banging on my door and said I was under arrest."

"Did he read you the Miranda rights?" Misty Dawn was betting that our illustrious county sheriff hadn't. "Wait! You don't live in the county, you live in the city. Why is the sheriff arresting you inside city limits? That should be for the local police to do."

Hubba Bubba wiggled his massive shoulders. "I don't know. Trixie lives in town also. I don't remember him reading me my rights. I'm always groggy when I wake up. I need like two or three cups of coffee before I really get going in the morning."

"Do you have an attorney?" I asked. I was getting tired of standing so I leaned back against the wall. Hubba Bubba was sitting in the one of the three chairs in the room. "If not, I'll get you one."

He shook his head.

"Don't say anything else except you want an attorney," ordered Rhonda Jean. She put her finger to her chin tapping it. Okay, that was a signal. "Ladies, five, four, three, two, one."

The guard came back in. "Leave. I gave you a couple of extra minutes."

Misty Dawn turned to him. "I'll let your wife know you were helpful, Randy."

He didn't blink an eye as he escorted us out. As we left the building Misty Dawn waved her forefinger in a big circling motion indicating we were gathering back at my house.

Our redneck monster black trucks with the gleaming silver trim left the parking lot just as Dimwit pulled in. It took a moment or two before he realized Misty Dawn had dared to trespass on his sacred ground. He did a u-turn in the parking lot almost sideswiping one of his own deputy's cars and flipped on his siren.

I grinned because this was going to be fun. I had actually practiced the maneuver we were going to do with the girls. Since I was the last and only inductee into the Lady Gatorettes, it was my job to slow down Dimwit as much as possible.

As he barrelled up behind me, complete with the flashing blue lights and blaring siren, I slowed down. I looked in my rear-view mirror and started to laugh. He was hunkered over the steering wheel, eyes bugging out, and his lips were in a thin tight line.

As he tried to go around me on the two-lane county road, I eased gently over into that lane. I kept glancing into the mirror as I saw him starting to go over in the other lane. I did the only thing that was appropriate in this situation, I moved over into that lane first.

I could see him forming words in the mirror, none of them could be used in a church setting. I laughed as I stuck my hand out the window and waved for him to go around.

Ever the adult, Dimwit gave me a three-finger salute as he passed my truck.

With the precision of a military drill team, each one of the girls' trucks ahead of me turned either right or left depending on the street. This left one lone truck going a few miles over the speed limit. Dimwit headed right to it with all the fervor of a hound dog treeing a raccoon.

As the truck pulled over, Dimwit did a slide in right behind it. Popping out of his car, he rushed to the driver's side.

Opening the truck's window, Flo smiled sweetly. "What did I do wrong, Dewitt?"

She said later he just stood there bug-eyed and didn't say anything for a moment.

"Where, where is she? Where is Misty Dawn?" He sputtered.

"We all had errands in town today, Dewitt. I'm not sure where she is."

He stomped back to his car and pealed out, according to Flo.

We were standing around in my kitchen a few minutes later drinking more coffee and laughing.

"Hey, quick question, why isn't everyone's truck Gator orange and blue?"

Rhonda Jean grinned. "Think about it, Parker. Those colors are way too easy to see at night. Black trucks are almost impossible to spot until you're right upon them."

I nodded, made sense to me. "Hey, anybody know why Hubba Bubba's sitting in the county jail versus being arrested in the city?"

Everyone shook their heads no.

Punching a number on my phone, I waited for an answer.

"Parker, it's always a pleasure. What's up?" The deep, smooth as velvet, voice of my personal attorney Robert greeted me. I quickly explained what happened with Hubba Bubba.

"All of this sounds like a set up to me. Can your plane be ready to go in forty-five minutes?"

"Let me text Missy. Robert, I'll have a car waiting for you at the airport. Black SUV."

I texted Missy. Then I called another number and leaving my message on her answering machine. "Hey, Celesta, it's Parker. I need your help on something important. Call me back as soon as you can."

Mary Jane waggled an eyebrow. "Really? Celesta?"

"Of course. That gal knows everything that happens in town..."

"Or thinks she does," snorted Misty Dawn. She had a love-hate relationship with Celesta.

I ignored her. "She'll know who to call to find out why Dimwit did what he did."

Celesta Summers was a former city commissioner who happened to be the only surviving member when a semi-deranged individual blew up city hall during a meeting.

Channelling her inner John Wayne, she had pawed through her oversized purse, found Mr. Smith and Mr. Wesson, jumped up on a pile of rubble, while screaming at what she believed was a terrorist act. It wasn't.

Celesta was a small, rock solid woman of indeterminate age with various shades of red, brown, and gray making their way through her hair.

She knew everyone in town and knew how to get answers inquiring minds needed to know.

"Hopefully, she'll call back within the next hour." You just never knew when she'd call back. It depended on her mood.

We chatted for a few more minutes and just as everyone was getting ready to leave my house, Pink's 'So What' started playing on my phone.

Grinning, I waved it in the air. "Hello, Celesta. Yeah, yeah, you, too. Hey, do you know anything about Hubba Bubba being arrested for Miss Trixie Delight's murder? By the way, I have you on speaker phone 'cas the girls are here."

Her voice was shrill. "That woman worked at that place of ill-repute. They have prostitution going on there…"

Rhonda Jean yelled, "No, they don't, and no one's ever been arrested for that there, Celesta!"

And let the games begin.

"They have drinking that goes on in there, naked women dancing, inflaming married men's lustful desires when they should be home with their wives." She continued to drone on while Mary Jane, Myrtle Sue, and Flo were trying to restrain Rhonda Jean from screaming at Celesta.

Misty Dawn and I rolled our eyes, semi-shaking our heads at the same time. "Celesta, all of that's very interesting but what about Hubba Bubba?"

Trying to get Celesta back on track when she was off on a runaway train was a wee bit of a challenge, but I usually just cut back to the original question and that seemed to do the trick.

"Well, Dimwit arrested him."

"I know that, Celesta." I managed to be somewhat civil. My sarcasm was overlooked. "Why him and not the police?"

"I have it on good authority," this meant someone in the police department, probably the assistant police chief, "that there was an anonymous call made from a burner phone to nine-one-one which, as you know, goes through the sheriff's department. The caller said Trixie Delight was dead, Hubba Bubba did it, and someone should arrest him before he escaped."

"Wait a second, Celesta. Hubba Bubba told us they woke him up and slapped handcuffs on him."

"That's true. Dewitt was in the bullpen and heard the nine-one-one call and decided in his typical fashion that he needed to go right then to arrest Hubba Bubba."

Her voice lowered. "I also have it on good authority that Dimwit didn't read the Miranda rights to Hubba Bubba. But now he, Dimwit, has a major problem with the Po Ho po-po and they're not happy with him. There's supposed to be a meeting tonight during the city commission as an emergency item."

She paused, "They're going to ask for his removal from office."

Whoa! That was serious.

"Let me talk, let me talk!" Rhonda Jean was almost foaming at the mouth. "They can't do that."

Misty Dawn turned around, annoyed. "Do what, Rhonda Jean?"

"He's an elected official. There's all sorts of protocols they have to follow before that can happen."

"She's right but they apparently have him on a number of different things. He's been warned before." Celesta reluctantly agreed with Rhonda Jean while giving us a further explanation of what was probably going to happen.

Ah, small town politics.

"Back to Hubba Buba, Celesta, I have my attorney coming down from Atlanta and he'll have Hubba Bubba out shortly."

"This is Po Ho, we don't like Yankees coming in and telling us what to do," huffed Celesta.

"Atlanta is the Deep South, Celesta, not New York."

"There's a lot of Yankees up there. Your guy probably has a Northern accent."

My patience level was starting to wear a little thin. "Celesta, let's get back to the topic. How was Trixie killed?"

"That ho." And that did it for me.

"Celesta, stop that right now. You don't know that, just give me the facts." I snapped.

"I looked her up on the we know people website and she has an arrest record a mile long." She was getting defensive.

"Celesta." I growled, rubbing my face.

"Okay, she was found in her living room with two glasses of wine on the coffee table along with a pink flamingo feather.

We all looked at each other.

"Are you saying Miss Maisy killed Trixie?"

"Wouldn't surprise me a bit."

CHAPTER 6

Celesta, you have finally gone off the deep end." Misty Dawn was laughing. "Flamingos don't drink wine and, more importantly, that silly bird couldn't gotten there by herself. Give us another theory."

There was a pause, I guessed Celesta was probably debating about whether to respond to Misty Dawn's comment about being off the deep end.

"That was Dimwit's theory."

"What's your theory, Celesta? I think you know something you're not telling us."

Another pregnant pause. "Rumor is she was dating...and I use that term loosely...David from The Capt'n's Table, and also Fat Freddy at the Burger Barn."

"So she wasn't being the faithful type of girlfriend Hubba Bubba thought she was then, right?" Flo was looking around and giggling. "Most guys are dumber than a box of bricks."

"So says the one who's been married umpteen times," snorted Mary Jane finally letting go of Rhonda Jean.

"Watch your mouth, missy!" snapped Flo starting to ease her way over to Mary Jane. "I'll bring Casper over to your house and let him visit you for a couple of days."

Mary Jane paled considerably. She was beyond afraid of Flo's snake. She didn't say anything else.

"Why was she dating other restaurant guys?" Misty Dawn was curious.

"Supposedly, and this is all rumor, she was going to take Hubba Bubba's flamingos and either sell or give them to one of her new boyfriends."

I shook my head. "Still doesn't make any sense. He was going to marry her. Why would she take the flamingos and give or sell them to another restaurant in the area?"

"Hubba Bubba said he had a bill of sale for those birds. I don't see how she could give or sell them to someone else. Just my opinion." Myrtle Sue had also let go of Rhonda Jean.

"Don't know."

"How was Trixie murdered?" I still hadn't gotten a real answer from Celesta yet.

"I guess she might have been poisoned. She wasn't stabbed or shot. Anyway, the city commission tonight is going to be fun for sure. Are y'all coming?"

"Maybe," I was cautious in my answer. "One last question, Celesta. Are you going to run for mayor?"

Since the unfortunate demise of all the other city commissioners and mayor during the untimely city hall explosion, the fine folks of Po Ho needed to vote all new people in. The upcoming election had very few citizens willing to serve. Pretty much whoever agreed to run would win that seat.

"No. I don't want the hassle. I liked being city commissioner, but I've decided I can be more effective as a private citizen versus an elected official."

"You can give them more grief and aggravation." Rhonda Jean was on a roll today. Maybe she needed a doughnut. I motioned to Mary Jane to look in the freezer. She knew what I meant.

Holding up my waffle box and shaking doughnuts out of it, I made a note to myself to just leave all doughnuts in their original box the next time I stuck the emergency sugary delights in the freezer.

Mary Jane popped them into a still cold oven. I guess they heated up when the oven warmed up. Since I'm not Martha Stewart I had no clue how it worked.

"You know, anyone can run as long as they have an in-town address. Okay, listen, I've gotta go but if I hear anything else, I'll let you know."

And she was off.

We looked at each other as the oven timer pinged. Yes, it was a lightbulb moment for sure.

CHAPTER 7

You know, sugar, salt, and caffeine are works of the devil, don't you?" Rhonda Jean was licking the doughnut sugar off her fingers. "Kidding!"

We all laughed. Looking like little swivel-headed evil Chuckie dolls, they whipped their heads around quicker than the scary exorcist movies from back in the day.

"Parker, you know how to do this." Rhonda Jean was wicked. My formerly hidden sense of debauchery was oozing its way to the forefront of my brain. My little hamster was bouncing up and down in his teeny-weeny little cage. I swear I could almost hear him laughing.

"Um, what do you mean, Rhonda Jean?" I was trying to play Miss Innocence.

"That's not a becoming look on you," grinned Misty Dawn pointing at me. "I can always tell when you're up to no good."

"Works on everyone but you guys." I semi-pouted but with a smile on my face.

"It's because we took the illegal but highly effective FBI secret course one of us may or may not have found on the dark web on micro-expressions."

"Yeah, whatever." My eyeballs had headed north in my head. "I'm pretty sure we can do this. I know I can get whatever documentation we need." I clicked on my phone to see what time it was. "Robert should be here. I'll ask him."

Flo patted her hair. "Is he bringing Hubba Bubba over here?"

"No, Flo!" Everyone shouted.

"Girl, have you no shame? Trixie's been dead less than twenty-four hours and you're already thinking Hubba Bubba is going to be your next husband? You are bad," admonished Myrtle Sue, a look of semi-disgust etched on her face.

"I never said any such thing!" Flo tried to look horrified at the suggestion but didn't quite pull it off. "He is a successful entrepreneur though."

"Pretty sure he's a 'Nole," winked Myrtle Sue, knowing full well that was the kiss of death for a die-hard Gator fan. Never shall the two mix or marry...well, at least not with the Lady Gatorettes. Oh, they were all for the Florida State Seminoles except when they played the University of Florida Gators and then they wanted the Gators to annihilate the 'Noles.

"No, he's not," snapped Rhonda Jean disgusted. "Everyone in this room knows he was a Gator linebacker including you, Flo."

She pouted. We ignored her.

Rhonda Jean almost spit the words out of her mouth. "Myrtle Sue, don't mess with Flo like that."

Myrtle Sue smirked.

"Um, do we really want to go through with this?" I could feel my heart beating a little faster, not with fear, nope, but with borderline eager anticipation of a lot of fun.

Whoops of "Go Gators!" and "Yes!" came from the girls. They proceed to dance around my kitchen. I don't think it was all from the sugar and caffeine either.

Grinning, I called Missy. "Hey, I need you to do the following ASAP." I proceeded to give her all the details.

"Y'all, I think we're in for a fun-filled ride." I lifted my coffee mug up in a toast. We touched our mugs gently. No point in breaking a cup and losing precious coffee.

Misty Dawn's phone rang. We snapped our heads around at hearing the unfamiliar song. No one ever called her including John Boy. She pulled her head back slightly, looked at caller ID, and frowned. "Speak." Her tone was frosty. Then she grinned. "Oh, hey, Mary Edith. How you doing? Yeah, I didn't recognize the number. Yeah, um, huh, really, that's interesting. I'll drop off a couple dozen brown eggs to your house later today. Thanks for letting me know."

She feigned a nonchalant expression and refilled her coffee mug.

It was quiet for a few minutes before Flo finally asked, "Well, what was that about, Misty Dawn? Since when do you ever drop off eggs to anyone?"

"That's irrelevant. Those chickens are producing like nobody's business out there on my ranchette. I have to get rid of them somehow and none of y'all complain about getting free eggs."

"The call, Misty Dawn, the call." Flo was impatient. The rest of us were too but in the interest of getting all of the information at one time instead of trying to pull it out of her we decided not to say anything...although it was annoying. Misty Dawn could be rather good at that.

"That was Mary Edith down at the supervisor of elections office." Pausing to take a sip of her brew, she continued, "Y'all know who Brandi-Lynn Hennessy is, right?"

Rut row. We all nodded our heads in the affirmative. We weren't fans.

"Turns out she's just filed paperwork to run for mayor..."

"What!" I exploded. I had to put down my cup for this choice bit of information. The other girls had a few choice words for this announcement.

"Wait, wait, wait!" Misty Dawn was enjoying her moment and was milking it for all it was worth. She was grinning. "Since no one else is ...theoretically... running, she would get it without anyone having to vote."

"That's illegal," Rhonda Jean's voice was crisp. "The woman is a convicted felon and I know she can't run for office anywhere in the state of Florida."

Her emotions took over and she sputtered, "Even here in Po Ho as mayor. How is she even doing this?"

Robert stepped through the kitchen door with Hubba Bubba who was staring at the coffee pot. Mary Jane grabbed two cups from the cabinet, filled them, and handed the mugs to the guys.

"She's probably basing it on the fact that she's suing the state for false imprisonment."

"Robert," I was annoyed, "the woman was convicted and served two years in prison, not nearly enough for what she did. She did the crime, she did the time, and she can eat the lime."

Robert smiled, his most becoming feature, and one that could make the most jaundiced female melt at fifty feet. I had seen him in the courtroom smiling at female jurors and watching them almost ooze to the floor. I knew his dentist made a fortune from making sure Robert's smile could be featured in a toothpaste ad.

"The city would have to take her to court, tying them up in a long, drawn-out, and potentially costly battle. Meanwhile, she would still be mayor until the whole thing blew through the court system, which, I might add, could take several years.

"Or they could just let her be." He smiled showing off his dimples. "However, I'm betting y'all have something up your sleeves." He looked over his mug with bemused eyes.

"Oh, I'm not finished." Misty Dawn wasn't impervious to Robert's smile; however, she didn't like the spotlight being taken from her.

We all turned our attention back to her. She nodded her approval, winked at Robert, and continued, "Brandi-Lynn now has a Po Ho address." Making air quotes, "She has moved in with her niece so said niece can attend cooking classes in St. Augustine."

"When did she do this?" I gritted my teeth.

"Supposedly, ninety days ago. The requirement is only sixty days."

Robert raised his eyebrows. "Really? That's it? Most places require a six-month residency."

We all lifted our shoulders in a don't know show of agreement. Mary Jane explained. "It's Po Ho, what do you want?"

I was busy texting Missy with new details. We had all pretty much ignored Hubba Bubba who was now sitting at the table with his coffee mug between his hands.

"Um, I'm hungry. Y'all want to come over to the fish camp and have dinner. It's on me."

Flo sashayed over to him, putting her hand on his shoulder. "Honey, that's awful sweet of you but Mary Jane has already sent out for pizza." She glanced over at Mary Jane who was now texting like the madwoman of Chaillot. I'm guessing she was telling the Pizza Palace to get a move on and probably offered a larger-than-normal tip.

Flo purred, her hand still resting on his shoulder, "We need you to stay here for a bit longer so we can tell you what we have in mind."

Hubba Bubba's eyes narrowed in puzzlement and then widened as he looked around at us.

"Not that, you twit," groaned Misty Dawn shaking her head. "Most of us are married and you don't want to mess with our husbands."

He did look a wee bit deflated and defeated. He spread his hands out on the table and muttered, "I didn't say nothing."

Misty Dawn nudged me. "Go ahead, Parker, and tell him what we're gonna do."

With a big cheesy smile on my face, I proceeded to tell him.

CHAPTER 8

Even Robert grinned at our plan. "You know, I actually think you can pull this off. What a hoot that would be. You would probably get national publicity from this."

"I still say we need to buy the Pizza Palace." Misty Dawn silenced Mary Jane with a semi-stern expression. "Other people in this town need to make a living, MJ, not just us."

"I hate being called MJ, Misty Dawn, you know that. Call me by my right name." She eyed Misty Dawn for a brief moment, almost daring her to say MJ again. "Rhonda Jean, tell Robert about your police scanner watch idea."

That took another thirty minutes. The good news was the pizza had arrived along with a copious amount of Coke and we were happy campers inhaling our pizzas and drinking Coke.

Hubba Bubba watched us in amazement as ideas flew back and forth between us. "I thought you girls was crazy, I'm convinced you are, but a good kinda crazy."

"Were," corrected Flo in a somewhat sultry voice.

"Were what?" He was confused.

"The verb for 'you girls was crazy' should be 'you girls were crazy.'"

"Okay." Apparently, he didn't understand the finer nuances of the English language or the correct verb usage. I was guessing he just didn't care since we understood what he meant.

"Robert, you have contacts for a legitimate company that would like to buy our idea, the watch and software, right?" Rhonda Jean was hopeful.

Grinning, Robert nodded his head. "Probably could get a positive response by this time tomorrow. How much do you think it's worth?"

The girls all pointed at me. Robert's smile got even bigger. "I can tell you before she even answers, it's going to be in the low..."

I tried to arch an eyebrow up. It was still a skill that I hadn't perfected yet because both eyebrows went up.

"Scratch that, probably in the mid-nine figures. If that's agreeable to y'all?" He showed off his pearly whites once again.

"We do that, we're going to need Joe D. to handle our offshore banking needs." Mary Jane was looking up Joe D.'s number on her phone. I, on the other hand, simply punched one number.

"Yo, Joe D., what you up to?"

Mary Jane glared at me with daggers in her eyes. She wasn't having a good day between me and Misty Dawn. She'd get over it, maybe, hopefully.

"By the way, I have you on speakerphone." I needed to give him fair warning so he didn't say anything lewd and lascivious.

Although he normally didn't do that, with my luck, this would be the one time he did. I shouldn't have worried.

"Hey, girls, how y'all doing? I'm assuming you're calling me about a professional matter."

Robert sang out, "Hey, Joe D., Robert here. We're going to need your assistance with some offshore banking. Think you're up to the challenge."

Oh, great. The alpha dog in both of these men was getting ready to come out and play.

Joe D. just chuckled. "How much are we talking about, Parker?" And just like that Joe D. took control of the conversation.

"Mid-nine figures." I'm pretty sure he could hear the grin in my voice.

"I'm assuming we're not talking about a million and change," he chuckled again.

"Nope."

"Of course, I can handle that. Would that be split between you and the other Lady Gatorettes or is it going to be one transaction?"

I looked at the girls who held up their first finger. That certainly would make it a lot easier for each of us.

"Split."

"Give me until tomorrow morning to look at a couple of options for you for the best rate of return but, yes, I can do that. Do you have a timeline on the funds?"

I looked at Robert. "Joe D., it probably will take a week or so, no longer than two weeks. I'll let you know the details as I have them."

"Parker, let's..."

"No, Joe D., talk to you later." I disconnected the call. The girls made kissy sounds. I suppressed my inner construction worker potty mouth.

Hubba Bubba had witnessed this entire exchange. Since I didn't know him that well and since he probably shared all sorts of information with whatever partner he was with at the moment, I was a wee bit concerned he might share our information.

A diabolical thought occurred to me. Maybe I've been hanging out with the Lady Gatorettes too much.

"Hubba Bubba."

He looked up at me with hopeful expectant eyes. "Yeah?"

"You realize you've heard way too much on our latest business venture, right?" I nodded my head up and down.

"Maybe."

"While you've been here with us, we've had cameras and audio installed in your house."

He jumped up. "That's not legal! Robert, tell them that's not legal."

Robert pretended to clean out his ears while looking around the kitchen. "Sorry, Hubba Bubba, I didn't hear anything."

It pays to have a good attorney on retainer.

I ignored his outburst. "If you so much as breathe anything about our latest business venture before it is closed, we will send over some very rude ex-special ops guys to visit you."

Pausing for special effect, "Sometimes it's a little hard to control their permanently destructive ways."

Poor fellow fainted. Hey, that wasn't my intent. I really just wanted to scare him, badly. I did but I didn't mean for him to flop out on my kitchen floor like a dead fish.

Ever the epitome of an unflappable attorney, Robert walked out the kitchen door.

Flo leaned over Hubba Bubba, tapped him on the shoulder, and murmured, "Do you think we should leave him here?"

"Oh, phooey," scoffed Misty Dawn waving her hand, "what a wimp! Do you really think we can trust him about the mayor's race?"

Rhonda Jean said, "Well, Parker did threaten to kill him."

Mary Jane started to giggle. "Guess he's never going to play never have I ever with us. Did you see the look on his face right before he fainted?"

We all looked at each other and did a silent Gator Chomp. The fear factor worked a little too well on Hubba Bubba.

He groaned and slowly turned on his side on the floor before opening one eye. "I want to go home. Will one of y'all take me home? It's been a really long day. I'm stressed and the love of my life is dead."

Oh, yeah, I guess we forgot about that. The emotional trauma he was suffering was real. Whether Miss Trixie Delight ever loved him was irrelevant, he definitely had had feelings for her.

But were we going to apologize for our behavior? Um, no. The better question is why would we start now? We weren't.

Flo did offer to take him home. Misty Dawn suggested, and I use that term loosely, that we draw matchsticks to see who would have the guilty pleasure of driving Hubba Bubba home. Myrtle Sue won. She's married and none of us had to worry about her intentions with Hubba Bubba.

It was a cleverly designed ploy to keep Flo from possibly throwing herself at him when he was in a vulnerable state. It was also getting harder to buy a wedding gift for Flo.

After umpteen marriages, I've lost count, but it could be as many as five, she couldn't walk into the local Target without one of the employees pointing at the wedding kiosk for her to register her gift list.

Flo watched Myrtle Sue and Hubba Bubba leave with a little smirk on her face. Maybe she knew Misty Dawn had probably rigged the matchstick drawing, I suspect not, but she and Myrtle Sue had not appeared to be on the best of terms recently. Maybe she was happy Myrtle Sue had left the premises. Some things are just better staying unknown.

"Um, something's really not right about this murder," she opined. "While our illustrious law enforcement departments are busy duking it out, why don't we figure out what's going on?"

She looked at us hurriedly trying to get a feel for the group. We all nodded in agreement. It was rare for Flo to take a leadership position.

"Let's go take a ride by Trixie's house, see what we can find, and then boogey on over to the city commission meeting." She paused, "Um, Misty Dawn, you might not want to be in the same room with Dimwit. It's going to be wild enough in there anyway much less without having him trying to arrest you."

Misty Dawn looked thoughtful for a moment, scrunched her lips together, furrowed her brow, and then nodded. "Think I'll go check out things at Fat Freddy's Burger Barn and then head over to The Capt'n Table to talk to David."

She looked at her phone. "Okay, we'll recon here once the meeting is over. Rhonda Jean, text me when you're leaving the meeting."

Oh, great, another late night at my house...and probably more pizza. I think I need to create an air freshener with the delectable aroma of pizza.

I needed to get these girls to eat something other than pizza or I was going to have to buy stock in Tums. Another naughty thought popped up in my head as an alternative. I smiled to myself while my little hamster started the spin cycle on his tiny wheel.

We decided to take two trucks to visit Trixie's house, that way Misty Dawn had her own vehicle to go visit Po Ho's fine dining establishments later.

Trixie's house sat almost in the middle of three large lots. It was white with green shutters and a hedge of azaleas fronting the house. If you thought of an old-fashioned seventies type of home, you'd be right. I was surprised. I honestly thought it would either be a hovel or a flash-and-trash type of mobile home.

There was a loosely draped yellow crime tape on the front door and that was it. Nothing to indicate a murder had occurred on the premises.

This was going to be easy.

CHAPTER 9

Pointing at the light over the front door, Misty Dawn said, "She has one of those ring video cameras. Wonder what's on it."

"Us." I poked her. "Let's see if there's a back door." I wasn't worried about our trucks being in full view of the neighbors if they looked out their windows. I was sure this wasn't the first time big monster redneck trucks had been parked outside Miss Trixie Delight's door.

Wandering around to the back of the house there was a screen enclosure, known as a bird cage in Florida, with an inflatable hot tub sitting on the concrete pavers. No crime tape was visible anywhere.

Misty Dawn tried the back door and discovered it was unlocked. Determining there weren't any cameras we could see, Misty Dawn motioned for us to come on in the house.

Flipping the kitchen light switch on, we discovered Trixie was apparently a very tidy individual. The kitchen was cleaner than mine; although, let me point out, she didn't have the Lady Gatorettes popping in at all hours of the day and night with pizza, Coke, or doughnuts.

Her living room was somewhat modest, but she did have a matching love seat, couch, and a theatre-style recliner along with a faux-marble coffee table. There were still the two wine glasses along with the pink flamingo feather on the table. Celesta's information was good. Believe it or not, Trixie's phone was still on the coffee table.

I shook my head, appalled at the inefficiency of Dimwit. One would have thought he would have collected the evidence instead of leaving it out in the open. No wonder the Po Ho police department wanted him removed from office.

"Um, shouldn't the police or Dimwit have taken all of this stuff to get tested for fingerprints or residue inside the glasses?" Mary Jane was a little baffled with potential evidence for Trixie's death being ignored by law enforcement. I could tell she was itching to pick up the wine glasses.

I was really hoping Flo wouldn't pick up the pink flamingo feather and stick it in her hair as a lovely new fashion accessory. One never knew what she might do.

"Yep." I answered looking around. "I'm guessing because he's at war with the Po Ho po-po and no one's taking over the investigation.

Rhonda Jean had pulled some cheap, dollar store, disposable plastic gloves out of her pocket and handed each of us two gloves.

"Wear these. We don't want our fingerprints anywhere. Misty Dawn, did you open the back door with your hands?"

Glaring at her for a moment, Misty Dawn shook her head. "I used my shirt tail to do that. Rhonda Jean, this isn't my, or even our, first rodeo."

Rhonda Jean grinned and did the Gator Chomp and thus eliminating any potential problems the leader of this caffeine-and-sugar infused group of hormonal women might have.

After being around them for a while, I don't think they're as much hormonal as they are from the sugar roller coaster of spiking their insulin into the stratosphere and then having it drop down into a mud bog but I'm not a doctor.

"Hand it here." Rhonda Jean stretched out her hand for the phone Misty Dawn had just picked up off the coffee table.

"Why?"

"Because I'm faster and better than you are about finding data on phones."

Misty Dawn shut her eyes, grimaced, tugged on her hair, and then held out the phone for Rhonda Jean to work her magic.

"Hey, you guys notice anything?" I looked around. They shook their heads no with a somewhat puzzled expression on their faces. "Sniff."

Everyone took a deep breath and slowly let it out. "Nothing, right?" I was almost gleeful. "Y'all are much better than I am about smelling stuff but there's not even the scent of anything in here including a stale smell."

Myrtle Sue lifted her head, shut her eyes, and took a deep breath. Then she started to walk slowly through each room in the house and came back as we were standing in the living room doing nothing.

"She's tidy."

"Yeah, we know that," I retorted. "What else?"

"The bathroom has an air freshener in it with a fresh ocean breeze. Her office had the slight smell of WD-40 but I think that's because she had sprayed it on the closet doors. Her bedroom had the scent of Gain laundry detergent. Her guest bedroom smelled the same way. There's nothing out of the ordinary here."

She walked into the kitchen and hovered her head over the garbage trash can taking a deep whiff of whatever was in there. "Something chemical is in here."

Mary Jane looked in the cabinet under the kitchen sink and pulled out a large black garbage bag. Flo found a pair of scissors in a drawer and cut the plastic bag along the seam on the side so it laid flat on the floor.

Myrtle Sue emptied the half-filled container onto the plastic. Carefully picking through the half-eaten container of yogurt, a couple of cans of no-salt vegetables, napkins and paper towels, she finally found the box of rat poison. Lifting it up gingerly, "It's basically a new box. Anybody see any evidence of rats or mice anywhere?"

We all scrambled in the kitchen opening cabinet doors. For whatever reason, Trixie, or whomever owned the house, had installed LED lights in all of the cabinets. This made it easy to see an entire area once the doors were opened.

We checked the enclosed back screened-in porch area as well as the rest of the house. Gathering back in the living room, Myrtle Sue finally announced, "Nothing. I didn't see any evidence of rats, mouse droppings, or holes anywhere did you guys?"

We all shook our heads.

"Whoever was here must have put rat poison in the wine and that's how Trixie died." Mary Jane eyed the wine glasses. "Betting you there's still rat poison residue in there and those idiots haven't tested it yet."

"Yikes!" exclaimed Rhonda Jean looking at her phone. "We need to get to the city commission meeting like right now."

Misty Dawn grinned and flicked her wrist at us to leave. "Y'all need to get on over there. I'll finish up here. Text me when you're leaving."

She was up to no good. Why inquiring minds want to know? Because she was just way too happy to have us leave.

We all tromped through the back kitchen door and jumped into Flo's truck aka the Black Beauty. She had named it after her favorite horse book as a kid.

Arriving at the Official River County offices, yes we had offered to let the city commissioners use our meeting room for free much to the chagrin of the real chamber of commerce, I noticed the parking lot was full.

After the chamber wars, we won by the way, B.P. Harris, the head honcho, still wasn't talking to any of us Lady Gatorettes willingly.

As far as we were concerned, we were doing more for the city and county than her good ole boy counterparts were. We had actually brought in more business to the area. The good news was even though we, myself and the Lady Gatorettes, owned the property and building, we had hired others to actually run our chamber. We didn't have to do anything except have a monthly meeting, they took care of everything else.

Our staff greeted everyone as they entered and directed them to our meeting room which could comfortably seat approximately sixty people. It was already packed. We always had reserved seating for any event in our meeting room.

Dimwit entered the room, eyed the fine citizens of our area, and his eyes quickly turned back to us. Marching over, he demanded, "Where is she? Where is Misty Dawn?"

Backing up slightly, I asked, "Why, Dewitt? You going to ask her for a coffee date?"

Mary Jane, Myrtle Sue, Rhonda Jean, and Flo snickered.

"Oh, look." Flo was going for the distraction effect with Dimwit. "There's Chief Ron. Yoo hoo!"

Honestly, I don't think Chief Ron had a clue as to who Flo was, but she was a cute blond and she was waving at him. I thought Dimwit was going to stroke out and die right there next to us.

His eyes bugged even further than they normally did, his head started to shake with fury, and his face pinched up. He snorted and then stomped off to the other side of the room.

This was going to be good.

CHAPTER 10

The city clerk Quenella, yes that is really her name and it's pronounced kwee-nella, was running the meeting until a new mayor and commissioners could be elected. Quenella is a very large lady who can put Whoopi Goldberg to shame with her very neat cornrows and length of dreadlocks. No fake weaves here.

Quenella was a creative soul at heart and decided if she had to work a boring government job then she was going to exhibit some color into her life.

Today, her dreadlocks where in alternating rows of orange and blue. Yes, she was a die-hard Gator fan and I dare say she suspected the Lady Gatorettes were going to be at the meeting. I'd like to think she did her hair color to appeal to them, but I knew better. If she had to rule on something between a Florida Gator and a Florida State University Seminole, she wanted people to know where her loyalties lay just in case anyone had any doubts.

Po Ho is a small town, people, this is one of the myriad of ways it is run...and, I dare say, in small towns across the country.

Quenella had been asked to run for mayor since she basically ran the city anyway. Her acerbic response was something to the effect of when pigs fly.

She motioned for me to come over. "Don't y'all start anything. There's going to be enough craziness with Dewitt and Ron."

I grinned, putting my hand on my heart. "Who? Us? Nah, we're not going to do anything. We came to watch the fireworks."

She agreed. "More than likely. Git on back to your seat and try not to aggravate Dewitt. I do have some first responders on standby in case he has a heart attack or something."

I scooted back to my seat and relayed Quenella's comments to the girls. I could see Dimwit out of the corner of my eye leaning up against the wall. He was more twitchy than normal. I wondered if there was any medication that could help him with that.

The first part of the meeting went smoothly. There were awards presented to an outstanding student from each school.

Quenella banged her gavel, "There's going to be a ten-minute recess before we start the next part of the meeting. Let me forewarn everyone there will not, repeat will not, be any form of confrontation prior to us coming back in here."

She looked at Ron and then particularly hard at Dewitt. "If there is any type of confrontation, verbal or otherwise, the offending parties will not be allowed to come back into the meeting."

Pausing, she eyed me and the girls. "For example, if Parker sitting over there," and she pointed at me, "got into a heated discussion with Mary Jane."

Oh, shish kebob, Mary Jane stood up and waved at the crowd invoking several snickers.

Quenella ignored her and continued. "Parker would be escorted out or not be allowed entry back into the meeting. I would rule in Mary Jane's favor on whatever it was she was bringing to our attention."

She gazed around the room. "Do I make myself clear?" Nodding, she banged the gavel down hard. "See ya in ten."

Quenella was a sweetheart, but you didn't want to cross her. As city clerk, she had seen her fair share of underhanded tactics, dirty politics, and general nastiness from both the adoring public and local politicians. She didn't suffer fools easily or kindly. She was, however, great at her job and got things accomplished.

We stood up and stretched. Rhonda Jean showed us her silenced phone. Misty Dawn had given a quick report. She was the soul of brevity. "Interesting info. On way to Captns."

Myrtle Sue mused as she waved to a couple of people in the audience, "Guess that means she's already been to Fat Freddy's and now going to The Capt'n's Table. How long you think the rest of this meeting is going to last?"

"Are we betting and what does the loser have to do?" I grinned. A nasty thought entered my mind.

"Buys pizza and doughnuts for everyone for a week." Mary Jane smacked her lips. Oh, this was almost too good to be true. I could wreak havoc with the girls. It was almost worth me losing; however, my natural competitive streak wouldn't allow that.

"Thirty-five minutes" was my guess.

Myrtle Sue thought it would be an hour. Flo guessed an hour and a half. Mary Jane was sure it would be forty-five minutes. Rhonda Jean had been doing some calculations on her phone, barely lifting her head, "It's going to be thirty-six to forty minutes."

Grinning to myself, I was actually proud that Rhonda Jean and my times were so close together. That girl could run calculations like nobody's business, and she was usually right. I was just using the guess and by golly method.

People trooped back in and took their seats. Quenella tapped her gavel. "Welcome back, everyone. We really only have one major thing to go over tonight. Each person gets seven minutes to state their case. Since I'm the one in charge until we have the elections for the new mayor and new city commissioners, I am the judge, jury, and final say so-so person. If someone does not like my ruling, take it up with the city attorney."

She paused, gazing over the crowd, "Let's start. Po'thole Police Chief Ron Wood is asking for the removal of River County Sheriff Dewitt Munster. Chief Wood, approach the podium and state the reasons why you think Sheriff Munster should be removed as sheriff. Keep in mind, this is a serious allegation of misconduct, and your statements are being recorded and videotaped."

Ron stepped over to the podium. He was definitely an imposing figure. Well over six feet tall and built like the former semi-pro football player he'd been in his early twenties, he also had the charm of someone who was used to getting his own way. Confidence oozed out of his every pore. His body language projected he knew he was going to win against Dewitt.

I think everyone in the room knew Dimwit was facing an uphill battle except maybe Dimwit. People had come for the fireworks.

"Good evening," Ron was surprisingly very soft-spoken. "I am fully aware that what I'm about to share is serious. I do not take this lightly. I have attempted on numerous occasions to work with our esteemed sheriff."

When elected officials start using words like esteemed or my colleague or anything along those lines it is equivalent to their being sarcastic and cursing at them in polite political language.

"Unfortunately, Sheriff Munster has allowed his pride, ego, and emotions to take over investigations.

"For example, months ago a member of a well-known ladies group was suspected of murder and subsequently cleared by a court of law and the FBI. Sheriff Munster believes an injustice was perpetuated and the said individual is still guilty of murder regardless of what the court system determined. As such, he regularly chases her vehicle, makes U-turns in the middle of heavily trafficked roads, has gone into a number of establishments in our community demanding to know where this individual is. This is continual harassment of one of our citizens who has contributed time and money to our community."

Did we know Ron was going to use Misty Dawn as an example? Nope. We were, however, nudging each other gleefully.

"On five other occasions, the most recent one just thirty-six hours ago, he has arrested people within the city limits when he did not have legal cause to do so. He is not authorized to arrest or interfere with any investigation we, the city police department, is working on.

"Every one of our investigations have to do with crimes being committed here within our city. Sheriff Munster was in the Public Safety Answering Center and heard all of the calls coming in on each one of these investigations. He decided to take action on at least five of these calls and did not notify the police department or me personally, to let us know he was on the way to the crime scene. Standard protocol is officers must make arrests only within their jurisdiction," Ron held up his finger, "unless there has been a previous agreement made between our agencies that officers can make arrests inside our city limits. We have never had an agreement between the county and the city."

Ron paused another moment for effect, "This is an egregious abuse of his office. He has arrested people who had nothing to do with any of the crimes committed. He has compromised numerous investigations. We've had cases thrown out of court due to his negligence of proper law enforcement protocol.

"This latest incident involves a well-known restauranteur who was awaken and arrested for the suspected murder of a woman here in town. Both of these individuals live within the city limits. There was absolutely no reason why our esteemed sheriff should have arrested a local businessman while he was sleeping when he had absolutely no proof this gentleman was involved in any way with the murder."

Quenella raised her finger indicating one minute left.

Ron nodded. "In conclusion, every arrest Sheriff Munster has made within city limits, he has failed, let me repeat that, he has failed to read the suspect's their Miranda rights, he has tampered with physical evidence, and has allowed others to possibly taint the evidence scene. Sheriff Dewitt Munster needs to be removed from his position as sheriff effective today!"

Dewitt was sitting in his chair, twitching, crossing and uncrossing his legs, gritting his teeth, and turning a lovely shade of fuchsia. I wondered once again if he was going to have a stroke.

Quenella nodded to Dimwit. "Sheriff Munster, it's your turn. Please step up to the podium."

Dewitt ran his fingers down the crease in his pants before walking over to the podium. Taking a deep breath and blowing it out through his nose, his normally high-pitched voice came out even squeakier. "It's obvious to me that this is a witch hunt. I can arrest anyone anywhere a crime has been committed."

I could tell Ron was having a hard time not to snort or otherwise attract Quenella's attention.

Apparently not recognizing the shocked looks on the citizens faces, Dewitt didn't realize he had once again shot himself in the foot...at a public forum no less.

"I'm not going to put up with your shenanigans, lies, and mistruths!" Spittle was forming on the corners of his mouth.

The crowd started to murmur. Quenella slapped the gavel down. "I told y'all to be quiet or y'all can leave." The group locked their lips tight.

"You people don't appreciate my years of dedicated service and hard work. I quit!" He ripped off his sheriff's badge from his shirt and threw it at Quenella striking her in the shoulder.

The crowd gasped. I was shocked. Dimwit had really lost control this time. Before Ron or anyone else could get up from their seats, Quenella had side-armed her gavel and struck Dimwit in the forehead whereby his eyes glazed over and he dropped to the floor.

Okay, I started to giggle a little. Hey, it was funny to see someone get hit in the head with a sidearm throw, especially from a seated position. I was impressed. Quenella obviously had talents I didn't know she had.

"Chief Wood, Sheriff Munster assaulted me and I want to press charges."

Nodding, Ron motioned for two of his officers to come pick up the limp form of Dewitt. As he became conscious and started to sputter, he was read his Miranda rights. There was absolutely no question about what was happening.

We were all in shock at Dimwit's total meltdown. I vaguely wondered who the next sheriff was going to be. It appeared the entire city of Po Ho's elected officials and a new sheriff was going to be decided by election within the next thirty days. The city was a ship without a rudder. Well, that wasn't exactly true. Quenella was still the one running things, and she wasn't about to let the city drown.

She clapped her hands for the crowd to settle down. "Now that y'all have had your evening's entertainment, we're dismissed."

People were chattering and texting like crazy on their phones. The newspaper reporter was almost running to her car with excitement. She had taken a lot of pictures of Ron and especially of Dewitt. She might have even gotten the money shot of Quenella side-arming the gavel at Dewitt. If she did, that photo was going to go viral on social media and maybe even the national news.

Jamie, the videographer, had already packed up his equipment and was hustling out the door. Oh, yeah, he had the video and it definitely was going to make the national news as soon as he edited it.

Just like that, once again, Po'thole was making national news. Seems like this poor town just couldn't catch a break. Yet on the glass is half-full concept, any national news caused people to come here and spend money, not a bad thing.

Rhonda Jean had already texted Misty Dawn. Meanwhile, I had slipped into my little used chamber office and made a quick phone call to the Pizza Palace. It was all I could do to keep from giggling as I met back up with the girls and we headed to my house for a recon session.

The fun was about to start.

CHAPTER 11

"**T**his isn't pizza!" Mary Jane spit out her slice and looked at it carefully. "What the heck is this stuff, Parker?"

"I think the Pizza Palace got our order mixed up with someone else's." Flo was almost whining after she had taken the first bite out of her pizza.

Rhonda Jean and Misty Dawn lifted up their pizzas from the individual boxes and looked at the bottom of the pizza.

"It's not pizza crust." Misty Dawn informed everyone. I was trying really hard not to laugh; however, tears were starting to head south down my face and my shoulders were shaking from unsuppressed glee.

"I'm not liking you very much at the moment, Parker," growled Rhonda Jean sniffing at her slice. "Mary Jane, what is this stuff? What's in here?"

"Cauliflower. They flipping gave us cauliflower crust!" She was shouting. "Parker Bell, what in fudge nugget hades did you have them do?"

Between gales of laughter causing my insides to exercise mightily, I managed to explain my cauliflower pizza crust decision. "I am so tired of eating pizza and doughnuts. I wanted something healthier, so I told the Pizza Palace to make the crusts cauliflower."

Wiping the tears from my eyes with the heels of my hands, "I thought it would be fun to try something new."

Myrtle Sue grumped, holding up her limp slice, "You thought wrong, although it really isn't that bad. I did see a recipe for it on the food channel."

"I'm going to order more pizza," declared Flo as she started to enter the numbers on her phone. "Myrtle Sue, don't even think about making it."

"Nah, just let it go. It's not going to hurt us to eat something a little different for a change." Misty Dawn was carefully looking her pizza over. "You didn't have them do anything else to the pizza did you, Parker?"

I shook my head. I continued to laugh. At least I was still in the land of the living.

"You're not getting a Gator Chomp for this," snapped Flo holding up a slice of pepperoni pizza and apparently debating about whether to ingest it or not.

Misty Dawn agreed with her. "Don't do this again, Parker, or it won't be pretty the next time."

A warning is a warning, but it was so worth it. To be honest, I wasn't wild about the cauliflower crust either, but I sure wasn't going to admit to that.

Amongst some groans, not happy ones, the girls finished up their pizzas and it was time for our debriefing.

Rhonda Jean brought Misty Dawn up to speed on the city commission meeting. She was beyond delighted she had been mentioned, although not by name, in Ron's talk.

We all agreed Dewitt had been losing what few marbles he had left in his brain for several months.

Mary Jane did have some compassion for him. "I hope he gets sent to a mental health rehab place so they can help him with whatever is going on in his brain. It might just be a chemical imbalance that can be helped with herbal supplements."

"Or drugs." Flo smiled and then hastened to add, "Legal ones, y'all, legal ones."

As much as Dimwit chased after Misty Dawn, she always considered it a game, she agreed with Mary Jane. "Yeah, he needs some serious mental health help. He can't ruin people's lives by arresting them on bogus charges. Does anyone know if he has family here in town?"

We all looked at each other. I didn't know. Myrtle Sue thought for a moment. "I know his mama died about five or six years ago, but I don't know anything else about him."

"When he came into the diner, unless there were other deputies with him, he always ate alone." Flo had once been a waitress prior to the success of the Lady Gatorettes radio and reality TV show.

"You know," mused Rhonda Jean nibbling the edge of her pizza slice, "I'm starting to feel a little sorry for him. Maybe he's been without family way too long and the pressure of the job just finally got to him. He just snapped out of reality and into an alternate world."

A sudden thought popped in my head. Before I could even get it out, I swear those girls can read my brain sometimes, Myrtle Sue spoke up with, "Not to worry, Parker, you're not going to be like Dimwit. You've got us."

All of the girls did the Gator Chomp. I was touched and had to turn my head so they wouldn't see my eyes glistening.

They like me, they really, really like me. Of course, if I ever ordered cauliflower pizza crust again, that sentiment would change…quickly.

"Okay, enough of our meeting. Misty Dawn, what went on with you?" Flo was eyeing her third slice of pizza like there was a lizard on it. I wasn't sure if she was going to eat it or not.

Misty Dawn replied, "That rat poison in Trixie's house wasn't all that old. No one saw anything to indicate that she had a rat or mouse problem."

Shaking our heads, Misty Dawn continued, "I held up the wine glasses and could see a little bit of some type of residue at the bottom of one of the glasses. I had an eye dropper out in the truck. I sucked up a bit of the residue and wine and put it in a bottle so we can have it tested."

She glanced over at Rhonda Jean who was nonchalantly eating her fourth slice of pizza. "Rhonda Jean."

She was ignoring Misty Dawn until Misty Dawn snapped, "Rhonda Jean!"

"Um, what, Misty Dawn?"

"Did you take Trixie's phone that was on the coffee table?"

"Um."

"That's not an answer." Misty Dawn was glaring at Rhonda Jean.

"Yeah, maybe," she muttered around the pizza in her mouth.

"Okay." Misty Dawn grimaced, putting her hands on her hips. "Did you find anything on it?"

"I haven't had time to really look at everything carefully, Misty Dawn. You know we went to the meeting and then came over here. I'll take a look at it first thing in the morning," she promised.

Misty Dawn stared at Rhonda Jean for a moment. "Good thing Dimwit didn't take it with him for evidence. No one knows it even exists at this point. Maybe we can find out what was going on."

She pointed a finger at Rhonda Jean. "I expect an answer by nine tomorrow morning. Mary Jane, make sure you have enough food here for breakfast."

I swear I don't know why these girls don't just move in with me. In some ways it would make life so much simpler. If that ever occurred, I strongly suspected I'd be following Dimwit to the loony bin to find my place in the real world.

I was hoping the girls would go home. I was tired and it had been a long day. Thinking I could ease them on out of my house, I should have known better, I announced, "Ladies, it's been an eventful day. Let's reconvene at nine tomorrow."

"Are you kicking us out?" Flo seemed to be shocked. She folded up her pizza box for the trash.

Deciding I finally needed to establish some boundaries within my own home, I answered with one simple word. "Yes."

The silence was deafening. Each Lady Gatorette picked up their pizza box and placed it in the black garbage bag. They were eyeing me somewhat suspiciously but left through the kitchen door without saying another word. Mary Jane took the garbage out with her.

My saying "Go Gators!" and doing the Gator Chomp was probably not a wise thing to do at this moment.

I went to bed.

CHAPTER 12

Pink's **'So What'** stared playing merrily on my phone. I rolled over on the bed to answer it only to discover Flo staring at me. I jumped. She turned down the volume on my phone.

Morning person I am not and I never cared about being Miss Congeniality prior to nine a.m. The LED clock on the nightstand with its bright red light let me know it was only seven a.m.

As anyone who knows me will tell you seven is only supposed to come once a day...and that's in the evening.

"What do you want?" I snarled at Flo. She obviously had been up for a while. She was wearing khaki shorts with a blue and orange Gator polo shirt. And, of course, no outfit would be complete without matching flip flops.

"You're out of coffee."

"Whaatt!" I semi-screeched sitting up. Looking over the edge of the bed, I was trying to find my fuzzy Gator bedroom slippers to slide my dainty little feet in.

Guessing I must have woken up the little hamster in my head because the little bugger was doing an Irish tap dance on his tiny wheel.

My head hurt from sitting up too quickly. "What do you mean I'm out of coffee?!"

"There's nothing in any of your cabinets." Flo shrugged, she wasn't as much a caffeine addict as the rest of the girls were.

"Mary Jane is supposed to make sure I have coffee and doughnuts at all times. She's fallen down on the job," I snapped. "Misty Dawn is going to be told about this."

Flo lifted her shoulders again. "Not Misty Dawn's house and we don't work for you."

Giving Flo the evil stink eye, which had absolutely no effect on her whatsoever, I shouted, "Get out! You can tell every one of the Lady Gatorettes not to come over here today."

Finding my slippers, I slid my feet into them. Flo was just standing there with a poker face.

"Is this about the cauliflower pizza crust last night or the fact that I wanted y'all to leave so I could get some rest?"

Flo just shook her head.

"Why aren't you leaving?" I snarled as I made my way down the stairs to the kitchen.

I sniffed just to make sure she wasn't messing with me about the coffee. She wasn't. I didn't smell any freshly brewed coffee pulsating through the machine.

Flo wasn't behind me. Maybe she went home, I kind of doubted that but you never knew.

I was mad about being waked up at seven a.m. I was mad that Flo was staring at me when I woke up. I was mad there was no coffee in the kitchen although I knew there had been some last night.

I stomped out to the pool deck, went to the pool bathroom, opened the cabinet door under the sink, and pulled out a food container with a five-pound bag of Delicious Dark.

Going back into the kitchen, Flo still wasn't around, I started a pot of coffee. While it was making, I went back upstairs and changed into shorts and a Gator tee shirt. Flo was gone or, let me rephrase that, she appeared to be gone. I looked out my bedroom window. I didn't see her truck. Maybe she had gone but I wasn't going to bet money on it.

Good thing I didn't because she was drinking my coffee when I came back in the kitchen. I glared at her. She handed me my favorite mug with coffee in it. I took a sip and continued to glare at her.

I was good at this game of not saying anything. Any government contracts I have ever secured had been won by my not saying anything in the meetings during negotiation time. I could outwait anyone.

After a good ten minutes, during which time we had both re-filled our cups while staring at each other, Flo finally broke.

"Don't you want to know why I came over so early, Parker?" She asked softly.

Silently high fiving myself for besting a Lady Gatorette on something and secure in the knowledge that I had once again outwaited the misinformed. I nodded.

Patting her blond hair, "I brought today's newspaper over so you could see it first."

My lips started to stretch, barely concealing a smile, my anger was rapidly thawing. "Really? Where is the paper?"

She pointed at the kitchen table. In my anger and caffeine-free early morning tirade, I hadn't noticed the daily paper on my kitchen table.

"Yep, we made the front-page news."

I grinned, nodded my head in appreciation, and did a high five.

"Flo, this is going to be good." I grabbed the paper and scanned the article quickly. "This is almost verbatim what we sent to the paper."

She started to laugh. "I know! It's perfect, Parker. The better news is it's just one candidate against each other. No runoffs, no debates, no nothing. Just a flat out whoever wins is the one who wins."

Drawing her eyebrows together, "You're sure about everything being legal?"

"Yep. Missy checked everything out. Robert checked all of the legal documentation. We're good to go."

Frowning slightly, I questioned her. "By the way, who was it who called this morning?"

Her lips turned up into another smile. "Me. I thought you had slept in long enough."

I wanted to hate her. I really did but she had brought the newspaper with the article we had all been hoping for.

"What about the coffee?" I still found it difficult to believe I didn't have any coffee in the kitchen.

"What about it?"

I gritted my teeth. "Let's try this another way. Which one of y'all took my coffee last night?"

She batted her eyes at me innocently. "You watched us put the pizza boxes in the garbage bag and we left. Seriously, Parker, I don't think there was any left."

Although I didn't one hundred percent believe her, I didn't think I was going to get any more information. Plus, I had a secret stash, or maybe two, none of the Lady Gatorettes knew about. Truth be known I had, cough, cough, actually run out on occasion when it was just me. I was never going to admit this to anyone, and this was the reason for my secret stash coffee hideaway.

I heard them before I saw them. Those big trucks do make some noise coming up my driveway.

"Oh, by the way, Flo. Where's your truck? I didn't see or hear it earlier." I looked at her over the top of my mug.

"I parked it behind the camouflage wall," she pointed at the wall we had erected to keep Dimwit from knowing when Misty Dawn was at my house.

It was a wall erected among the natural foliage of azaleas and other green bushes. I don't know the name of them. Florida ugly green bushes is the term I use.

We, mostly Mary Jane and Myrtle Sue, had intertwined fake leaves and other artificial foliage stuff throughout the wire-mesh wall so it looked completely natural while providing a great cover for the girls' trucks. Martha Stewart would be so proud of us.

Walking through the door carrying groceries, Mary Jane sniffed. "Coffee?" She was a wee bit puzzled. Aha! That was the culprit who had stolen my coffee. Mary Jane would pay, and it wouldn't be cauliflower pizza crust either. Let the games begin.

"Have y'all seen the paper yet?" Flo was waving the newspaper around. "We need to call Hubba Bubba and let him know."

Rhonda Jean, our ever-brilliant master strategist, tittered, "The real question is how is Miss Brandi-Lynn Hennessy going to respond when she sees the paper, especially when she didn't think anyone else was going to run against her?"

I held up the newspaper. "Maisy Byrd, you are going to be the next mayor of Po'thole."

CHAPTER 13

The Gator Chomp was done by all of us while laughing.

Taking an educated guess your eyebrows have headed toward the North Star almost creasing your forehead, I'll answer the burning question that is probably playing in your mind.

Yes, Hubba Bubba's prized pink flamingo, Miss Maisy, is running for the public office of Po'thole mayor.

After paying Robert an exorbitant amount of money to examine the legal ramifications of having a non-human run for office, he discovered nowhere in the bylaws of the city or in the supervisor of elections office documentation anything that said a real live human being had to be the one running for office. The basic requirement was they had to live in the city for a period of sixty days before they could run for office, and they had to be over eighteen.

Miss Maisy met all of the requirements needed, she was twenty-one and a half, according to the documentation Missy and Robert had presented to us. The paperwork was all in order.

Hubba Bubba had supplied us with the bill of sale Trixie had given to him. Surprisingly, the dates actually corresponded to what we needed.

In another ironic twist of fate, he kept a wading pool in his back yard. That was Miss Maisy's real home, according to our very quietly submitted paperwork to the supervisor of elections office which is the information the newspaper used to verify her address. She would occasionally sunbathe and have some of her meals there. Her real job was a model in the entertainment industry. That was true, she strutted her runway walk every day at Hubba Bubba's Fish Camp Restaurant.

Hey, a girl's gotta do what a girl's gotta do to make a living.

Her last name Byrd was just a different spelling of bird...which is what she was.

The article in the paper highlighted her community activities. What was her participation in Po Ho and River County you ask?

She welcomed newcomers to the community. That was accurate. She didn't bite, spit, growl, or otherwise have any problems with any of the other flamingos once they were in her marshy pond area.

She created an atmosphere of love and peace with everyone who approached her. True, although a fence did keep her from her adoring public.

Hubba Bubba always maintained it was for her safety and not for those overly enthusiastic folks and small children who wanted a close-up selfie photo with her.

She promoted tourism for the area by making various appearances in the county as well as in town. Having people flock to Hubba Bubba's Fish Camp did constitute public appearances which could count as tourism. A little bit of a stretch but not a whole lot.

And the coup d'grace was she had never been arrested. She had never spent time at a government-sanctioned stay-cation resort...which the newspaper took great delight in pointing out to the voting public.

I'm sure Brandi-Lynn Hennessey was not going to be happy about that little dig about her in the paper.

Never once did the paper ever mention Miss Maisy Byrd was a flamingo. The Lady Gatorettes and I were sure the paper had no clue one of the mayoral candidates was a bird. Even if they did, they weren't fans of convicted felon Brandi-Lynn anyway.

Photos weren't required to run for office. I dare say the public had absolutely no idea they were going to be voting for a pink flamingo.

To say Brandi-Lynn wasn't well-liked in this area was an understatement. Especially since she had stolen, yes, she was convicted on this, funds meant for children with cancer in this area.

While Po Ho was economically disadvantaged, otherwise known as a po' area, the townspeople were quite generous in helping those less fortunate.

None of us were going to say anything about Miss Maisy and Hubba Bubba had promised not to based on the implied threat of death by one of the girls. Really let's just call it a vicious fabrication of truth that had the desired effect on him.

Pink's 'So what' started playing on my phone. Grinning, I waved at the girls to calm down. Missy was on the phone.

"Hey, Parker, you're never going to guess who just called that newly setup phone line for your candidate."

"Humm," I tapped my finger to my chin, feigning puzzlement although Missy couldn't see me. "I'm guessing Brandi-Lynn or one of her associates."

I heard a snicker. "Sometimes you're just no fun to play with, Parker."

"Yeah, I know. I've heard the rumors. What did she have to say? By the way, I'm putting you on speaker phone. My tribe is here."

Wrong thing to say. Shouts of "We're not a tribe" just about deafened my eardrums.

"Sorry, sorry." I amended my faux pas to "The Lady Gatorettes are standing next to me."

"I figured that out." Missy's dry wit could be annoying on occasion. We won't talk about my sense of humor. "She wanted to know what Maisy's qualifications were. I asked if she had read today's newspaper and she hung the phone up on me."

High fives and the Gator Chomp made for a happy moment.

Disconnecting Missy, it was time for serious business. I nodded to Misty Dawn hoping she understood what I meant. She did.

"Rhonda Jean, what did you find on Trixie's phone?"

Rhonda Jean was in the middle of putting a doughnut in her mouth and stopped mid-cram.

"Seriously, Rhonda Jean!" snapped Mary Jane glaring at her. "Put the rest of the doughnut in your mouth. I don't want to see your tonsils."

The rest of the girls nodded in agreement and resorting to consuming sorta, maybe, somewhat dainty bites of their doughnuts. None of the girls liked being called out for their lack of social manners.

Rhonda Jean swallowed, pushing her head back slightly to make sure the doughnut went all the way down her throat before answering. "Turns out Trixie had a lot of pies she had her fingers in."

She licked her fingers. "Before I go any further, Misty Dawn, you never told us what you found out from Fat Freddy and David."

Misty Dawn frowned. "Didn't I?"

We all shook our heads. Maybe she forgot. Unlikely.

She wiggled her eyebrows. I'm so jealous. "Fat Freddy says he was dating Trixie on the days she got mad at Hubba Bubba which was a couple times a week. And, yes, he was fully aware she was dating Hubba Bubba, but he didn't care. As he said, 'she was a lot of fun and could tell great jokes.' He said he only texted her but no calls."

"He's lying," stated Rhonda Jean looking around for another doughnut. Mary Jane handed her one.

"I figured as much. Anyway, David at The Capt'n's Table said he was in negotiations with her for some pink flamingos for his restaurant."

"Geez, Louise," harrumphed Flo daintily licking sugar from her fingers, "how many flamingos does this area need?"

Myrtle Sue shook her head as she washed her hands in the kitchen sink. "The better question is where was she getting all of these flamingos? Doesn't it seem strange to any of y'all that we might have a lot of those pink birds up here? I know we only have four or five really cold days but there's a reason why flamingos live in South Florida."

She had a good point.

"Also, don't exotic birds have to be examined by a vet?" asked Mary Jane as she looked in the doughnut box to see if there were any more.

Snapping my fingers, I dialed my vet friend Dr. Leah. I explained our questions about flamingos. There was a slight pause before she answered, "Parker, why don't you come in so we can discuss this in person."

That was a little weird. "Okay, I'll be there in about an hour."

I was curious about Dr. Leah's short conversation, but I was more interested in what else Misty Dawn found out from David.

Saving me from asking more questions, Flo arched her eyebrow, leaned forward, with a slight smirk. "What else, Misty Dawn? That couldn't have been all."

"Nope, you're right. He was also seeing Trixie on the side. He only knew about Hubba Bubba and not about Fat Freddy."

"Man, she got around," interrupted Flo as she was still holding one of her doughnuts.

"That's not all either. Wait until it's my turn again." Rhonda Jean had the grin of a Cheshire cat plastered on her face.

Misty Dawn continued, "Also, David paid her twelve thousand dollars up front for two pairs of flamingos that he never received."

"Whoa!" I was surprised he was stupid enough to pay for the birds up front instead of paying half and then the balance being paid once he received the flamingos.

"Yeah, and you're going to love this. He paid her in cash."

We were all in shock.

"Shish-kebob macaroni!" exclaimed Myrtle Sue. "Was David a special kind of stupid or what?"

It was safe to say we were all flabbergasted.

Misty Dawn continued on, ignoring our outburst. "Oh, it gets even better. Trixie didn't deliver on the flamingos. David had a fit and wanted his money back. Since it was in cash, I'm guessing you can figure out what happened next."

"Um, let me guess." Like, duh, was the answer easy or not? "Trixie said what money and David had absolutely no proof that he had ever given her the cash. He probably didn't even have her sign a receipt saying he had given her twelve thousand dollars. Bada bing, bada boom!"

Flo interrupted me, "Strong motive for him to kill her."

We nodded in agreement.

She was playing with her blond hair, twirling it around her first finger. Flo had never played with her hair when it was longer but since she now had a cute bob, she played with it all the time. It was annoying.

"Did he have an alibi, Misty Dawn?" She was still messing with her hair. I couldn't stand it any longer.

"Flo, please stop messing with your hair. It's making me crazy." I was trying to be reasonably nice about my request.

"Or what?" She got a little feisty. "You going to kick us out again?"

I groaned. This was not a win-win situation. Best I just let this battle go.

Misty Dawn did not step up to the plate to help me out on this. She ignored us both. "Fat Freddy was at his restaurant where a boatload of people saw him. He says he's on the store's video camera all the time except when he went to the restroom.

"David, on the other hand, says it was his evening off and he went home to watch some game on TV."

"He doesn't have an alibi then," flatly announced Mary Jane, her eyes flat. "Who else has reason to murder Trixie?"

"Who owns Babes, Babes, and More Babes?"

My eyes blinked wide open. I swiveled my head around to look at Rhonda Jean who was licking some unseen doughnut sugar off her fingers.

"What? I have no clue." She started tapping her phone. "Let me see if I can find anything out but it's probably buried under several fictitious names, and it can be a bear on locating that type of info."

Looking up from her phone, "Can't you get Missy to do it?"

Aarrggh! Of course I could but I didn't necessarily want my company resources to be tied up doing that. Reluctantly, I texted Missy with the request. She responded with several question mark emoji's. I sent it back with a Nike swoosh logo...Just Do It.

"You know your office can find it faster than I can." Rhonda Jean was trying to sound helpful. It didn't work. I gave her the stink eye.

As always, that had zero effect on any of the girls. I'm not even sure why I bother trying to do that.

My hamster was spinning merrily away on his tiny little wheel. Sometimes a reason or thought would come to me and explain my behavior. Nothing was coming up. Maybe my hamster had gotten fat somehow and was spinning just for the sake of doing something. I shook my head quickly and he stopped.

Rhonda Jean turned to Myrtle Sue who was starting to clean up the kitchen. "Does your hubby know who the owner is?"

She shook her head no. "I'm under the impression it isn't anyone local 'cas I asked him one time and he said he'd never seen the owner."

"I'll ask John Boy to ask some of the dancers..."

"Professional entertainers," quipped Flo doing a little pirouette. I snickered.

Misty Dawn kept on going. "I'll ask him to find out. Betting you they only have a manager, and he may not even know. It's worth a shot though."

She texted him. "Says he'll go tonight. Parker, he wants to know if he can take Denny with him."

My eyes crossed. "What? I'm not Denny's babysitter or his secretary. Tell John Boy to contact Denny directly. Besides which, I thought they were best buds."

She shrugged indicating she didn't care one way or the other. I didn't text Denny either. They're big boys, they can figure stuff out on their own.

"Maybe we should take some of the entertainers to lunch and see what they know," suggested Myrtle Sue. "They might be receptive to us being nice to them."

Flo snorted, "They'll see it for what it really is...we're trying to bribe them with food for information. I'm taking bets on how long it will be before one of them tells us they'll exchange information for money."

Misty Dawn actually bobbed her head up and down vigorously. "Don't let your head explode, Flo, but I'm agreeing with you."

In typical Flo dramatic action, she clasped her hands over her chest and announced, "Oh, be still, my beating heart. Misty Dawn just said I was right."

Misty Dawn grumped, "Not exactly what I said but if it makes you feel better about yourself, that's fine."

"Close enough," grinned Flo, patting the tops of her shoulders.

"Hey, I need to go see Dr. Leah. I'll catch you guys later." I was heading out the door when Mary Jane shouted out, "Hey, Parker, I'm fixing chili for dinner tonight. No pizza."

"Sounds good to me." I needed to hustle to see Dr. Leah. I wonder why she couldn't tell me anything over the phone.

CHAPTER 14

Arriving at the modest but exceptionally clean vet clinic, the vivacious Velvet ushered me back to one of the empty examining rooms. Dr. Leah came in, shutting the hallway door and then the door back to where all of the girls were working and doing their magic with the various animals.

"Wow! You've lost some weight."

Dr. Leah smiled proudly. "Yes, indeed, I have." A slight frown, then, "Parker, I didn't want to say anything over the phone because I think it's being tapped."

"Really? Not being mean here, Dr. Leah, but why would someone want to tap a veterinarian's phone?"

Looking a little distraught, she replied, "Doesn't make any sense, does it? I typically see dogs, cats, and other small animals. Anyway, I got a phone call several weeks ago asking if I knew anything about flamingos."

My eyebrows shot straight up and little goosebumps started to make my arm hair stand straight up. I leaned forward to make sure I heard her every word very clearly.

"I told them..."

"Male or female, Dr. Leah?"

"It was a female." She was a little anxious but continued, "I told her I knew very little about flamingos but what could I help her with. Her next question was would I be willing to stay after normal hours to take a look at a few flamingos. She said she was willing to pay double what our normal emergency rates are."

Dr. Leah paused, "I asked her if the birds were sick, and she said no. She needed a vet to say they were in good health. I reiterated I know very little about flamingos and, other than a cursory examination, that would be all I could comment on. She suddenly became very abusive, used foul language, and said I'd be sorry for turning her down."

Looking down at her hands for a moment, "Parker, I never said I wouldn't look at the flamingos. I just don't know a whole lot about them. I was going to suggest she go to the exotic bird vet in Jacksonville, but she had already hung up the phone on me.

"The next day I came in and Marie handed me a new cell phone. I asked why I had a new phone. She said a messenger had brought it in and said it was an upgrade. I didn't think anything about it but..."

"Let me guess, you started noticing little glitches in the phone. Like maybe, a funny echo sound or something like that." I knew who I could get to look at the phone and see if there was anything wonky with it. "Dr. Leah, do you still have your other phone?"

She nodded in the affirmative.

"Go back to using that one and let me borrow your new one for a day or two. Let me see what I can find out."

"Here's the thing, Parker, why would someone want to tap my phone? I'm a vet, it's not like I have some big national secret or anything and if I did, I certainly wouldn't discuss it over the phone."

I was puzzled. It didn't make any sense. I scratched my head as I was thinking. The little hamster was slowly starting his warm-up routine on the little wheel. An idea was slowly forming in the back of my mind.

"Dr. Leah, do veterinarians receive notices from the state on stolen animals?"

"No, there'd be too many of them."

"What do you think is going on?"

Dr. Leah stood there for a moment, appearing to be thinking and at the same time debating with herself on how to answer me. "Flamingos this far north in the state don't typically do very well because it does get cool, cold here. There's a lot of care and work that goes into taking care of flamingos."

"And?" I knew she wanted to say something else but was hesitant.

Taking a deep breath and slowly exhaling it through her nose, "I wonder if this person is trafficking them. Flamingos are expensive to purchase. If someone stole the birds, they'd be worth a lot on the open market IF you could find a buyer."

"Can they be tracked? You know, like with a microchip?" I didn't know.

"They can be but unless they're in a zoo or maybe a tourist attraction they probably wouldn't be."

She looked at the clock on the wall. "Last thing, then I need to get back to work. Here's the bells and whistles question, why me and why did the gal on the phone want me to look at the birds after normal working hours? It makes no sense unless they were stolen."

She opened both doors and indicated to Velvet she was ready to see another beloved pet. "Velvet, give Parker that new phone so she can have one of her people find out why the signal keeps going in and out. Make sure my other phone is charged up." Turning, she winked at me.

I left with what appeared to be the latest smart phone. Thing was it felt a little heavier than my phone. Rather than calling Rhonda Jean, I texted her the little face with a hand over its mouth emoji. "Check for bugs." She responded immediately with a thumbs up.

As annoying as cell phones could be, I was happy to have one.

Although I'm tone deaf, have no sense of rhythm, and know most of the words to any song that came on the radio that didn't stop me from singing. I have four notes I can sing on key but they're not necessarily in the same order.

If someone was listening in on Dr. Leah's phone, they'd simply hear me singing gustily off-key. It suddenly occurred to me my beautiful voice might be recognized by whoever was listening in, although they deserved what they heard in my opinion, but I decided to stop singing until I got back home.

Carrying the phone into my kitchen where I saw the girls were finishing up the remainder of fresh pizza, Flo pointed at an unopened box on the countertop. I immediately put my finger to my lips and walked out through the sliding glass door to the pool deck. Coming back in, "You were saying."

Flo pointed again at the unopened box. "There's yours and before you ask, no, we didn't order the cauliflower crust for you."

I grinned. "You're so kind."

Bringing the girls up to speed between bites of the loaded supreme pizza, "I'm thinking Trixie may have been the ringleader on selling stolen flamingos."

Misty Dawn had finished her pizza and agreed, "That or she figured out a way to make money and not have to deliver any product."

"But she did, allegedly, provide services," tittered Flo. "Those were some expensive services. Men."

"You would know," snipped Mary Jane. "You've been married enough times."

"You're just jealous!"

An ear-piercing whistle destroyed the somewhat peaceful tranquility of my kitchen. I put my hands over my ears. "Was that really necessary, Misty Dawn?"

"Focus, people, focus. Get back to the task at hand." She held up her hand, ticking the following off one by one on her fingers. "Why is Trixie dead? Who wanted her dead? Who owns Babes, Babes, and More Babes?"

Rhonda Jean was sitting at the kitchen table tapping on her phone. "Okay, we know Hubba Bubba didn't kill her. We know someone probably put rat poison in her wine glass. This means she knew the individual and trusted them enough to come into her house and have a drink with them. Fat Freddy isn't really a suspect, but David could be."

Mary Jane cut in with, "Maybe some of the girls from the club."

"Possible." This was from Misty Dawn. "It could be someone we don't even know about yet."

"Um, could it be a woman who put the rat poison in her drink?" Myrtle Sue looked around the room. "It seems to me it could be a woman. Men would do something bloody, like using a knife or a gun. A woman would do something sneakier, like using pills or rat poison."

That was certainly a thought. Before I could develop my thought process around the psychology involved on that, Flo popped up with, "It wasn't Celesta."

I couldn't help it, an explosive guffaw escaped from deep in my lungs and out through my mouth. "You're right about that. She wouldn't be caught dead in Trixie's house."

We all had a good laugh about that.

"By the way, Parker, while you were gone, I called over to Babes and told the dancers we'd take them to lunch tomorrow at Hubba Bubba's." Flo was carefully examining her bright red polished nails. She was the only one of the Lady Gatorettes who proudly embraced her girly-girl gene.

I mentally shook my head. I was doubtful we'd get much info from the strippers, pardon me, exotic dancers but, who knows, we might.

We agreed to meet at Hubba Bubba's at noon although Mary Jane informed us she was cooking breakfast once again at my house. We needed John Boy's report from Babes, Babes, and More Babes.

I swear there's a conspiracy in the air surrounding Po Ho. Nobody, no one, nothing wants me to sleep in past seven a.m. I don't care how much coffee is infused into my veins, seven in the morning shouldn't even exist; however, ALL of the Lady Gatorettes have an unshakeable belief that particular time constitutes mid-morning.

As far as I am concerned, it's a punishment from the Big Man Upstairs. I guess I've made one too many jokes about Baptists or Presbyterians or churches in general and I'm being punished.

This morning Potus blew his hot, semi-foul smelling doggie breath on my face. This was not my idea of a wonderful wake up call. His cold wet nose nudged me on my face. Ugh!

Groaning, I got up to see Myrtle Sue holding a cup of coffee in her outstretched hand. Potus, with his stinky doggie breath, contaminated my olfactory sense since I couldn't smell the delicious bean juice.

Gratefully taking the cup from Myrtle Sue, I raised my eyebrows questioningly.

"We're waiting on you to come downstairs." She left my bedroom, and I could hear her walking down the stairs.

Potus just sat there looking at me. "What? You live with Denny now. Leave me alone."

I think he understood what I was saying because he smiled that German Shepherd smile with his tongue hanging out and then turned around. I could hear his toenails clacking on the steps.

Groaning after taking another sip of coffee, I put on my Gator tee shirt and a pair of shorts and found out I had apparently opened a restaurant during the middle of the night.

Natch, all of the girls were there including Denny and John Boy. They had that "we've been up all night" look and proud attitude.

Whatever had been going on between them was resolved. Nothing like a little male bonding at your local strip club. Their bloodshot eyes gave the impression they were probably still feeling the effects of whatever they had consumed in the last twelve hours.

Mary Jane was slinging corned beef hash, potatoes O'Brien, bacon, toast, scrambled eggs, and doughnuts out on the countertop, family style dining at its finest. Everyone had grabbed a paper plate and was loading them up in case the national food supply chain suddenly stopped and we were on the verge of starvation.

Mary Jane handed me a filled plate so I didn't have to fight through the hordes of so-called friends who would probably kill me to get to the food.

I sat down at the kitchen table, eyed my food, and then dug in. Eating pizza and then chili last night in no way, shape, or form curbed my appetite for a new day. I did, however, have incredible heartburn.

"Wanna know what we found out?" grinned Denny. He was slightly swaying on the bar stool at the countertop.

"I'm sure you'll tell us," I muttered while chewing my food.

John Boy swiped his hand through his dirty blond hair to get it out of his eyes. "Yep, we found out the owner of Babes lives somewhere in the state of Florida."

We all groaned. Really? We knew that.

"So what, John Boy?" Misty Dawn sounded a wee bit testy this morning. "Did you get a name for us? Where they live? A corporate name by chance?"

"Um, no." He had a relatively shameful expression on his face. "We did find out that Trixie wasn't particularly well-liked by the other girls."

"Because she was always horning in on their guys," volunteered Denny. He was still swaying although not as much. "She'd flounce over to the guys and, basically, push the other dancers out of the way. This cut into their tip money."

Taking a big gulp of orange juice that Mary Jane had just set in front of him he continued, "There's no love lost with any of the girls that she's dead. They also think she was somehow scamming the guys she was dating."

John Boy jumped into Denny's conversation. "Yep, they said she was making good money dancing but a couple of months ago she suddenly started demanding more money as a dancer."

"Hubba Bubba told us she had offers from all over the country to go dance. Was that true?" Rhonda Jean had a big plate of food plus two doughnuts on it. Her left arm was wrapped around the plate protecting the food from either escaping or keeping everyone else at bay so they wouldn't attempt to take it. She didn't look at the guys, she was busy eating.

"According to one of the girls, I don't remember her name, Trixie was either hiding from someone or she was getting ready to go to greener pastures and that was the reason why she needed more money."

Since many strippers made lousy choices when it came to men, it wasn't hard to believe Trixie wanted to go elsewhere.

"Any clues where she wanted to go?" asked Misty Dawn reaching for John Boy's doughnut on his plate.

"Vegas."

"Well, of course, that's where all the professional entertainers go to make it to the big time." Flo could be really sarcastic at times and snickered. She was picking at a sprinkle on her doughnut.

Denny hiccupped, "She was good, but she wasn't Vegas good. She'd never work the strip as a lead dancer. She'd be dancing at clubs off the strip."

I was curious. "What happens to strippers when they get too old to, ah, perform?"

John Boy eyed Denny waiting on his explanation. "They get low-paying jobs most of the time or hook up with a scumbag for a less than desirable life." Denny shrugged. "Most girls in places like Babes usually don't end up with a happy life. Low self-esteem makes them targets for those types of guys you'd never take home to your mama."

Pretty much what I suspected. "What else did you guys learn?"

John Boy chortled, "They water down their drinks including the beer."

Misty Dawn lightly slapped the back of her erstwhile husband's head. "How much did you spend, big boy? So far, the info you've given us isn't worth a whole lot, probably not as much as you spent."

"You wanted information, Misty Dawn," he whined rubbing the back of his head. "We had to pay different dancers to see who knew what."

She growled. "I asked you a question, John Boy. It wasn't difficult. How. Much. Did. You. Spend?"

He turned to Denny. "Help me out here, bro."

Denny grinned stupidly. "See? There's a reason why I'm not married."

Turning to Misty Dawn, "I'll answer your question. He spent about two hundred dollars, and I spent the same amount, but we didn't have any lap dances. It was all to watch the girls and drink beer."

"Seriously, John Boy? Two hundred dollars on some ugly old girls shaking their taa-taa's and hineys around?" Misty Dawn was frowning at the back of his head.

I was biting my lip to keep from laughing out loud. No wonder they were still feeling the alcohol effects even with diluted drinks.

Four hundred dollars was a lot of money. Chances were they had tipped very well. There's a name for men like that...whales.

Knowing these two bozos as well as I did I was sure they were out to impress the pole swinging, mostly clothesless, dancing females. They probably thought they could buy the needed information.

Much as I hated to admit it, that was pretty darn close to what we were going to be doing at lunch time. The only difference was we'd be out in the daylight and not spending anywhere close to what the guys had.

Plus, chances were Hubba Bubba was going to give us free lunches. After all, his favorite three dancers were going to be eating lunch at his fine establishment where they could visit their pink flamingo namesakes.

It was a win-win situation. Hopefully. Maybe.

Mary Jane had started to clean up the kitchen. "Misty Dawn, I think you need to take John Boy home and let him rest up from his all-night factfinding mission."

Misty Dawn glared at Mary Jane who stuck her tongue out. They both chuckled.

Denny yawned, "I'm going to sleep in your guest bedroom, Parker. I shouldn't be driving."

I pointed down the hallway. "Go. Drink a glass of water before you lay down."

He nodded and toddled off down the hallway with Potus right on his heels.

"John Boy, please tell me Potus didn't go into Babes with you guys." I certainly hoped not.

"Naaa, he sat out in the truck and guarded it."

Misty Dawn cleared her throat and pointed at her husband. "I'm taking this one home. I'll see you guys at Hubba Bubba's around noon."

She escorted her still wobbly husband out to her truck. We watched as he struggled to get into the passenger seat. Misty Dawn finally shoved him in.

Flo giggled. "You know whatever she says to him on the way home he's not going to remember, right?"

We all nodded knowingly.

CHAPTER 15

I arrived first at Hubba Bubba's. Jennie, our waitress from the last time, hurried over to greet me. No doubt in my mind she remembered my very generous tip and was expecting more of the same. She would be right.

All of us in the Lady Gatorettes tipped well, although I strongly suspected the girls did it to make up for their wild and wooly ways while creating havoc wherever they were. Me? I did it to be nice and help improve someone's day who was working hard AND at a job I didn't want to do because I simply didn't have the temperament for it. I truly appreciate good service.

I told Jennie there were probably going to be ten to twelve of us for lunch. I preferred to eat out on the deck but that was subject to change. She nodded and hustled off to arrange the tables to accommodate us.

Standing next to the wooden railing, I was admiring the beautiful pink flamingos. They were so royal in their demeanor, so relaxed and peaceful. I vaguely wondered what that would feel like in my life.

Shaking my head to clear out that type of thinking, I knew I'd never read...or apply...any self-help techniques along those lines. If my therapist in Atlanta couldn't get me to do it, I realistically wasn't going to start here in Po Ho.

She had contacted me a couple times since I had moved back here and let me know she could conduct sessions via Zoom or Facetime. I turned her down and realized I had just been using her as a friend in Atlanta since I didn't have any outside of work.

Here, I have friends. Yes, they are all loose cannons with a wicked sense of humor, they're crazier than looney tunes, they're redneck smart, have a take-no-prisoners attitude, and they were fun. They had my back, and we were friends. Plus, I was the only inducted member into the Lady Gatorettes apart from the original members.

Perhaps I broke the mold on that because they swore they would never, ever again add a new member to the group.

Jennie waved me over to the table. "Hey, Hubba Bubba's here. You want me to go get him for you?"

"Sure, why not?"

A few minutes later, Hubba Bubba was gracing my presence while grinning like a monkey with a handful of peanuts. "Yo, yo, what's happening, girlfriend?"

That expression coming out of a very large man's mouth was disconcerting, but funny, at best.

I told him about everyone getting together for lunch.

He swiped his right hand through his curly red hair and was wearing a hopeful expression. "So, Miss Lexi, Miss Diamond, and Miss Pinkie are coming? Do you think they'll be impressed I named my flamingos after them?"

I smiled. "I would be. I'm sure they'll think very highly of you for doing that. You've honored them."

His eyes moistened. "Lunch is on me today. Just make sure you tip Jennie well."

"Of course!" Really? Did he think I wouldn't? But, then again, it's Po Ho and maybe he had to remind other patrons to take care of their waitress properly.

"Parker," he leaned in close to my ear so no one else could hear, "Your attorney Robert got all of the charges dropped but no one seems to know anything else about Trixie's murder."

The moisture in his eyes had grown and were threatening to spill down his cheeks. I guess he realized that wasn't going to be a good look while he was hovering over me. He straightened up and dug the heels of his hands into both eyes stemming the potential waterflow from north of his nose.

Leaning back down next to my ear, he whispered, "I can pay you girls to find out what happened to the love of my life."

Oh, wow! Hubba Bubba had it bad for Trixie. He probably was going to be devastated with what we knew already. Now was not the time to share it with him.

"Hubba Bubba, we actually need to ask you some questions about Trixie. You going to be around after lunch?"

"Yep. Y'all have Jennie come find me when you're through. We have a private meeting room, and we can talk in there."

The Lady Gatorettes descended in force on the deck.

"Hey, hey, big man!" shouted Rhonda Jean. "What's the special for the day?"

Jennie approached Rhonda Jean smiling. "We have several. Did you want to wait until the rest of your party arrives?"

I knew Rhonda Jean probably wanted food right at that moment but in the interest of being somewhat polite, she declined.

Her eyes darted around the deck, "Where are the, um, other girls?"

Hubba Bubba had been intently watching the parking lot, grinned, and pointed. "Here they are."

Their approaching the restaurant look liked a Coke commercial in slow motion. They were walking in unison, slowly tossing back their long wavy hair, and wearing happy smiles.

Wearing borderline Daisy Dukes and red-and-checkered blouses with the shirttails tied in a knot showing off their tight midriffs they advanced to the restaurant.

Spinning around on a pole tightens the abdominal muscles I guess...or they go to the gym a lot and I kind of doubted that.

When they spotted Hubba Bubba, they squealed with delight and hustled over as fast as their stiletto high heels would let them.

Surprisingly, not one of them tripped, fell, or otherwise turned a perfect ankle in the sandy parking lot. Must be all of the exercise they get in perfecting their stroll on dimly lit stages.

"Ladies, ladies, I'm so glad you came," gushed Hubba Bubba. He swept his hand toward the flamingos. "Did you know I named my beautiful flamingos after each one of you? There's Miss Lexi who has beautiful eyes like you."

I have to admit Miss Lexi did have beautiful green eyes and they weren't the contact green ones either.

"Miss Diamond who has the same dazzling smile as you do." These girls were practically swooning as Hubba Bubba described what he liked about each girl.

"And Miss Pinkie," he blushed, "has the same light pink color as you."

No wonder these girls liked Hubba Bubba. Not only did he treat them with respect, a gentleness that only certain men seem to possess, and he named his tourist attraction flamingos after them. Thus, ensuring their names would live as long as the birds did, a legacy for sure.

They all hugged and kissed on him while men at other tables showed definite signs of being jealous. Their wives and girlfriends, eh, not so much.

"Y'all have a good lunch. I need to take care of business." Hubba Bubba took off for the kitchen

The Lady Gatorettes all introduced themselves, and then it happened.

Mary Jane asked the one question we actually wanted to know the answer to. "What are y'all's real names?"

I guarantee you this wasn't the first time any of these girls had been asked that, probably by men and not women.

"Oh, honey, you don't need to know that. We're just plain old boring girls except when we're performing." Miss Diamond smiled showing off the same type of pearly whites that my attorney Robert had.

"If we told you, everyone at the grocery store would start calling us that and it would not help our celebrity status." This came from Miss Pinkie.

I was surprised none of the Lady Gatorettes said anything. I could see them thinking though, and that wasn't always a good thing.

"Um, Miss Pinkie," I was curious, "do y'all work in one place for a while and then move on? How does that work?"

She blushed slightly. "It's like any other job. You work somewhere for a while and then went you get tired of it, you go somewhere else or get another job."

Jennie took our orders and disappeared into the restaurant.

Misty Dawn smiled at the dancers. "I'm guessing y'all know why we asked you to lunch."

Miss Diamond had a throaty laugh. "I'm guessing it's not because you want to become dancers or want to learn how to swing on a pole in your bedroom."

We all grinned and shook our heads.

"Diamond, Lexi, and Pinki, tell us about Trixie. Why do you think she was murdered?" Misty Dawn would have made a fine prosecutorial attorney. She would have also made a great Marine.

Lexi answered first. "She never worked and played well with others."

"Meaning us," interrupted Miss Pinki as she daintily took a sip of the fish camp's ungodly sweet, iced tea.

"Well, except for men." Miss Lexi ignored the interruption and continued. "She'd come barging over when we were doing, um, personalized dances for the men and basically pushed us out of the way while continuing to entertain them. This cost us our tip money."

"We get minimum wage," explained Miss Diamond. "Tips are how we live."

"How can you make enough money to live on?" Myrtle Sue's eyes were wide. "Po Ho's not that big."

"We only dance Tuesday, Wednesday, and Thursdays here. Friday and Saturday we perform in Jacksonville."

"But we live here 'cas it's cheaper," clarified Pinki, "even with the gas prices, it's still cheaper. Plus, we commute together."

Misty Dawn got back to the topic at hand. "Did any of y'all want to kill Trixie?"

"We didn't like her but none of us are going to jail for her murder," murmured Miss Pinki. "She wasn't worth it."

Rhonda Jean now had a heaping full plate of fried catfish. Holding up one of the filets, she wiggled it, "How long had Trixie been working at Babes? Where did she come from and what did you know about her?"

Miss Diamond answered while forking a shrimp in her scampi sauce. "She was from somewhere down close to Miami. She had a lot of connections in that area and went back about once a month.

"I'm not sure what her real name was. It might have been..."

"It was Barbara Ann." This was from Miss Pinki.

"I thought it was Annie Mae." Miss Diamond glanced over at Miss Pinki.

She shook her head. "Annie Mae is Tina Turner, Diamond."

Miss Diamond shrugged. "Don't know her real name then and, before you ask, I don't think I ever heard her last name."

The other two girls shook their heads no.

"I know she'd been performing at some private club down south and said she got tired of it. She wanted to go to Vegas and dance. Po Ho was just a stop until she got there."

"Okay, I don't understand how all of this works," stated Misty Dawn, doing her Columbo imitation. "Why go from a large city to where you could make a lot more money to a little hinky dinky town out in the middle of nowhere unless you were hiding from someone? Why didn't she just go to Vegas and by-pass Po Ho?"

Miss Pinki smiled. "Sometimes you just gotta do what you gotta do to make money. Maybe she was leaving an abusive relationship and this was as far as she had gas money. I don't know. She'd only been here about four months or so."

"She'd been performing for a while," volunteered Miss Lexi taking a bite of her hushpuppy. "She had all the moves down, but she didn't have that something extra that we have."

They smiled proudly. "We're the real reason why guys keep coming back to Babes," Miss Pinki blushed. "It's not because of Trixie. She only went after the guys she thought had money. I think she thought they were going to be her way out of dancing."

That explained Fat Freddy, David, and Hubba Bubba.

"What about Trixie having offers from all over the country to come dance?" Misty Dawn was asking great questions that our inquiring minds wanted to know.

"It doesn't work that way unless you've got some big names or connections behind you," answered Miss Lexi. "When you want to change clubs, you just go to a new one, do a dance, and either they hire you or they don't. That's how ninety-nine point nine percent of us get gigs."

Miss Diamond sniffed, "Trixie didn't have that type of star power contrary to what she made Fat Freddy, David, and Hubba Bubba believe."

She smiled her million-dollar asset. "Yeah, we knew about all three of those guys. Mainly because she kept rubbing our noses in the mud saying she knew how to get them to give her money and making them think she loved them."

"So, was she a player or a manipulator?" Rhonda Jean was now on her third or fourth fried catfish filet. I had lost count.

"Both." All three said in unison. "But more of a manipulator than anything else." This was from Miss Pinki.

"Who owns Babes?" I asked quickly changing topics to see if I could catch them off-guard.

All three shrugged. "Don't know. I only know the manager Tommy and I don't even know if he knows."

I looked at Miss Lexi carefully. "Why wouldn't the manager know who the owner is?"

"Think carefully about it, Parker. Most of these businesses have, shall we say, less than desirable owners who may have nefarious connections. We don't need to know who the owners are, we just have to make sure we get paid."

Suddenly a light went off in my brain. My poor little hamster may have just gotten fried. I held up my hand and my eyes narrowed. "Wait a second. Where did you go to school?"

The Lady Gatorettes looked at me like I had lost my mind. This was the thing that kept tugging at the back of my brain. None of these girls talked like they had an uneducated background. Using words like nefarious did not come from a trailer trash homelife.

I was always under the impression most dancers at strip clubs were uneducated and were only wearing next-to-nothing strings of clothing because they couldn't do anything else. These were not those type of girls or maybe my thought process was totally in error. I didn't think so, but it was possible.

They sat still and didn't look at each other. My brain was piecing together information. I waved my hand for the Lady Gatorettes to continue to ask questions. I motioned that I was going to the restroom.

As soon as I was out of earshot, I called Missy, told her what I needed, and headed back out to the porch deck.

Almost as soon as I had sat down, my phone vibrated. Quickly looking at it, I confirmed what my brain cells had been trying to tell me.

The three dancers barely glanced at me when I sat down continuing their conversation with the Lady Gatorettes.

Not even acknowledging me when I sat down, Rhonda Jean's text read, "What u got?"

Looking up, I asked, "So, how's your psychology doctoral thesis going...Darla, Tammy, Charlotte?"

Before they could respond or even answer, the Lady Gatorettes all leaned forward, in unison, and asked the most important question of all. "Where are you going to school?"

God help the poor girls if they answered Florida State University derisively nicknamed Free Shoes U by Gator fans everywhere.

"I wondered how long it was going to take you to find out," voiced Miss Lexi as she put down her fork and watching us to gage our response.

"Which one are you?" Mary Jane's eyes were darting back and forth between the dancers or maybe I should say the post-graduate students. Humm, I wonder what they actually identify as?

"I'm Darla." Pointing at Miss Diamond, "That's Tammy and Miss Pinki is Charlotte. However," she acknowledged each of us by eye contact, "please do not use our names out in public anywhere."

Misty Dawn was tense and enunciated her question very carefully. "Where did you go to school?"

"Let's put it this way, since you've never seen our show, the orange and blue colors are front and center."

The tension immediately dissipated and the world in Po Ho was right again.

"Are you dancing to put yourselves through school or is it for your dissertation?" Mary Jane was thoughtfully staring at the girls.

Miss Pinki/Charlotte kind of laughed. "Probably a little of both. I like the money but's not something I want to do on a long-term basis. My thesis is 'A Hangout with A View' and how the exotic dancers perceive their clientele, both male and female."

"Mine is on 'Power and Authority in Strip Clubs,' volunteered Miss Diamond/Tammy. "This is a little different from a corporate business structure but close enough for a parallel to be drawn."

We all turned to Miss Lexi/Darla waiting. Smiling, she bowed her head, lifted it up and winked at us. "It's nothing along the lines of these two brainiacs. Mine is 'Proxemics and Kinesics – How Close is Close Enough in Gentlemen's Clubs?'"

I said the only intelligent thing I could think of at the moment. "Do what?"

Myrtle Sue stroked her chin. "I went to junior college, and I don't know what that word prox something means."

Miss Lexi giggled. "I didn't either when the professor mentioned it. I had to look it up. It basically means how much space you put between yourself and another person, different space requirements depending on specific situations."

"How long have y'all been dancing and how much longer are you going to keep on doing it?" Flo was quizzical but the errant thought occurred to me she might want to try it.

"Um, Flo, no." Yes, those words actually slipped out of my mouth.

Shaking her head, "Nope, not going to. I'm not shaking my taa-taa's for men to stare at. I'm curious as to the performing lifespan of an exotic dancer."

"I can answer that," responded Miss Pinki, "it's from whatever age you start to about thirty, maybe mid-thirties depending on how you look, move, etc."

"We've only been dancing about six months," twinkled Miss Lexi's green eyes. "We were friends in class and decided to do this together. It's also a safety factor for us to live and commute together."

Miss Diamond continued with, "We're only going to do this maybe another month and then that's it."

She shuddered, "I don't think I can stand any more men drooling over me."

Flo perked up. "That's not a bad thing, honey."

Miss Diamond retorted, "It is if they're paying money to see you dance and they think they want a little something extra…"

"Which we don't do," added Miss Lexi quickly.

Misty Dawn tapped the table with her knuckles. "All of this is very interesting; however, it doesn't help to find Trixie's killer and we also don't know who owns the club."

Miss Pinki looked at her watch, "Ladies, we appreciate lunch. Don't know that we helped you all that much, but we have things we need to get done prior to our dancing in a couple of hours."

The dancers stood up, thanked us once again, and sashayed their way back to their car.

Jennie was suddenly standing at my elbow. "Y'all through or do you need anything else?"

"Just let Hubba Bubba know we're finished." I stood up, "We'll see him in the reserved room." I discretely handed her two very large bills with the picture of the idiot who stood on a rooftop with a kite during a thunderstorm. She was very happy.

The Lady Gatorettes and I moved indoors to the reserved room where Hubba Bubba met us and closed the door.

"I can pay y'all to find out what happened to Trixie." He announced as he was clasping and unclasping his hands. He was upset.

Rhonda Jean took control of the group and held up her hand. "Stop right there, Hubba Bubba. While we all appreciate your very kind offer, we're not doing this for the money."

Jumping right in, Mary Jane pronounced, "We're doing this because we're friends."

Although the girls always came across as hard-nosed, uncaring, and non-compassionate women, the fact was they were kind, they were compassionate...to the right person, and they liked helping to solve murders and keep the citizens of Po Ho as safe as they possibly could. Me, on the other hand, tended to attract murders much like moths to a brightly lit light bulb.

This declaration of our friendship evidently caused Hubba Bubba to lose what little control he had over his emotions to spill forth from his eyes and down his cheeks. The poor man sat down in one of the chairs and started silently sobbing with his shoulders hunching up and his head in his hands.

Flo stood up and went to give him a conciliatory hug when Mary Jane grabbed one of her arms and jerked her back into the chair.

"Oh, no, you don't, Flo! You best leave him alone," she hissed.

Myrtle Sue had already wrapped her arms around the large man dwarfing her even more. She was softly murmuring into his ear.

"What about her?" squeaked Flo giving the evil eye to Myrtle Sue.

"She's married and there's no way he's going to misinterpret her intentions." Mary Jane grinned. "Yours, not so much."

"You're a royal pain," grumped Flo as she re-positioned herself in the chair.

Misty Dawn had been watching her motley crew much as a new mama duck does with her ducklings. Clearing her throat, "Hubba Bubba, what do you know about Trixie's background? Where was she from? What jobs has she done in the past? What was her real name? Was she dating anyone other than you?"

I held my breath on her last question, hoping he'd say yes; otherwise, the rest of our time together wouldn't be pretty. Heartbreaking for him would probably be an understatement.

Getting himself under control while taking a deep breath and slowly letting it out, "I just knew her as Trixie. It never occurred to me that she might have another name."

Seriously? As many gentlemen's clubs as he had frequented it never crossed his mind that the dancers had real names and that their stage monikers were fake? Unbelievable.

He continued. "She was from somewhere down near Miami, but it wasn't Miami. I don't remember exactly."

Blowing his nose into a paper napkin, he said, "She told me she didn't have much of a home life, she hated school, and knew she could make money dancing. One of her mother's boyfriends had told her that. In fact, I think he got Trixie her first job."

We almost jumped out of our chairs shouting, "Where, Hubba Bubba? Where was her first job?"

He had a puzzled expression on his face. "I'm, I'm not sure. Maybe it was called The Cabaret or something like that."

"How long ago, Hubba Bubba?" Rhonda Jean was poised over her phone ready to find the information via Google.

"A couple of years ago."

My little hamster jumped up and down on his tiny little wheel while spinning to the moon. Miss Trixie Delight had been out of school a lot longer than a couple of years. I vaguely wondered if Hubba Bubba actually had a clue as to her age.

"Got it." Rhonda Jean was so good at finding information quickly.

"You've got a picture of Trixie, don't you?" I asked.

"Yes, of course, I do." He pulled his phone out of his back pocket, asked for my number, and texted it over to me. I sent it to Rhonda Jean to see what she could find out.

"I think dancing is the only job she ever had. She said she had only been doing it for a couple of years. She was only twenty-two."

When he said that not only did I have the effect of spouting water from a whale but so did Mary Jane, Flo, Myrtle Sue, and Misty Dawn. My iced tea almost snorted through my nose. Rhonda Jean was busy on her phone.

If Trixie were only twenty-two, she was a very hard twenty-two. From what I had seen of her, she was a hard thirty or maybe even older.

I swear, what is wrong with men? Can't they tell a gal is aging when their eyeliner gunks up in their eye wrinkles? Even I can tell that and I'm not adept in the makeup department.

Trixie was a lot older than those college student girls. I started to say something, but Rhonda Jean cut me off. "I'm on it, just give me a minute."

"Something wrong with the tea?" Hubba Bubba was eyeing his tea quizzically.

We shook our heads. "Parker's wearing some type of perfume and we got a big whiff of it."

I can't believe it! He bought that stupid answer because he just nodded. I don't wear perfume...ever!

"Nope, on your last question, Misty Dawn," he said shyly. "She told me I was her one and only truly. She wasn't dating anyone else."

Oh, man, did I ever feel sorry for this poor guy. He was going to have his heart broken even more than what it already was. Trixie had played him like a puppy with a new bone.

"Um, do you know who owns Babes?" I'll give Misty Dawn credit where credit is due. She never let on what we knew about Trixie and busting Hubba Bubba's opinion of her.

He frowned for a moment. "No, I don't believe I do. Whoever the owner is it's probably buried under a boatload of shell corporations. I know Tommy's the manager but he's not the brightest bulb in the box."

I started talking to my little hamster who was spinning happily on his teeny tiny little wheel. *"Really? After what Trixie has made him believe and you're saying that Tommy's the dumb one."*

My little hamster apparently agreed because he slowed down for a moment and then speeded up again on tiny little wheel. Note to self, why am I talking to my little hamster?

"How did you get Miss Maisy?" Flo was smiling seductively. We couldn't stop her from doing that unless we duct taped her mouth and that really wasn't an option.

"Trixie had gone down to south Florida to see her cousin Jack who had cancer. He needed money for his treatment, and he had this flamingo for sale. Trixie said it was the only thing he had left that was worth anything. If I bought the flamingo, she could have it brought up here, I could use it as a tourist attraction and bring more business into the restaurant. Plus, it would help Jack with his cancer treatment."

I had to give Trixie kudos for her moxie. She played on Hubba Bubba's sympathies and compassion to help another fellow human being out.

There might be a Jack in her background somewhere, but I seriously doubted he was a cousin with cancer. I also doubted he needed money for cancer treatment.

"Um, Rhonda Jean." I tried to get her attention.

Never looking up from her phone, she acknowledged me with, "Told you, I'm on it. You gotta give me a couple of minutes."

Properly chastised once again, I decided not to ask her any more questions.

Flo was being gentle. She spoke softly. "Honey, you do know flamingos aren't allowed to live at people's houses, don't you? Only zoos and some tourist attractions are allowed to own them."

Hubba Bubba shook his head. I could see it in his eyes that he knew Trixie had swindled him, but he simply wasn't going to confess to it. If he admitted that, then he was probably going to have to concede she pulled the wool over his eyes on a number of things as well, including his heart. I don't think he was prepared to do that.

"She said her cousin had caught Miss Maisy in the wild..."

"Illegal, Hubba Bubba, and you know it," blurted Flo slapping her hands down on the table. "You can't take exotic wild birds from the Everglades, assuming there are even that many anymore, and keep them as pets. The state of Florida will be all over you."

He became very defensive, crossing his arms over his chest and leaning back in his chair. "You know what? I didn't care. If her cousin needed money for cancer, then I could help him out.

"Having Miss Maisy here for a couple of weeks was good and the fact that Trixie brought in three more was even better. Miss Maisy was starting to get a little cranky being by her lonesome all the time."

Sounding more authoritative, he uncrossed his arms and placed his hands on the edge of the table. "Did you know flamingos are very outgoing birds? Did you know they need to have other flamingos around them to be happy? Did you know zoos usually have a flock of ten to keep these delightful pink creatures happy?

"And, before you ask, yes, I was going to buy six more birds. Why, you ask? Because they are beautiful. They're pink, they stand on one leg which most of us can't do for very long, they have soulful eyes, and they have long, graceful necks. Plus, they seem to hug each other a lot and have a really cool looking courtship thing they do. This is really good for my business."

"They're expensive to buy and maintain," pointed out Myrtle Sue.

Hubba Bubba shrugged, "So what? I can afford it."

"Do you have the proper permits?" I was still wondering about the legality of what Trixie had told him.

He shrugged again, "Trixie was working on it. Said Jack was looking through his paperwork."

"Aha!" announced Rhonda Jean triumphally. She held up her phone. "You're not going to believe this."

CHAPTER 16

Unfortunately, I could believe almost anything at this point. The rest of the girls were doing side eye glances at each other. We probably all suspected the same thing.

"Go for it." Hubba Bubba looked smug, hands clasped in front of him on the table. Frankly, it appeared he was having an employer-employee discussion with us instead of finding out the so-called love of his life had defrauded him, cheated him out of a lot of money, and had lied out the wazoo to him.

Rhonda Jean plastered on her I-know-more-than-you-do smile. "There was a flamingo stolen from the Miami Zoo three weeks ago. Kind of looks like Miss Maisy, doesn't it?" She held up her phone for all of us to see. Hubba Bubba just blinked and didn't say anything or turn colors.

Carrying on, she tapped on her phone going to another page. "And here, in lovely Palm Beach, three more of the dainty pink birds were stolen just last week. Is it my imagination or aren't they Miss Lexi, Miss Diamond, and Miss Pinki?"

There was a knock on the door. "Come on in," shouted Hubba Bubba. It was Jennie.

"Um, there are six more flamingos being put in the pond. You might want to come out here and see them. The guys say you have to sign the paper saying they've been delivered."

Rut row! Maybe Hubba Bubba was behind the flamingo acquisition and not Trixie. Although he wore his emotions on his sleeve, he was a very smart guy and a good businessperson.

While I was thinking, all two seconds of it, the girls were scrambling out the door as fast as they could. Hubba Bubba had a slight frown on his face as he trailed behind them. I was the caboose.

Sure enough, the same guys we had seen a week earlier delivering Miss Lexi, Miss Diamond, and Miss Pinki from the back of a U-Haul truck were off-loading six more birds. Four were slightly larger and I surmised they were the males.

Hubba Bubba ambled over to the guys, appeared to sign some sort of document, and headed back to us.

"What did you name these?" harrumphed Mary Jane disdainfully.

He grinned, seemingly carefree about the arrival of the probably stolen flamingos being delivered to his business. "John Boy, Big T, J.W., and Danny. The last couple is Randy and Miss Giggles."

"Whoa!" screamed Rhonda Jean advancing toward him. "You can't name those birds after our husbands!"

Wearing a smarty-pants smarmy grin, he said, "Just did and it's listed on the bill of sale like that also."

Oh, my golly gee, that slimeball basically just convicted John Boy, Big T, and J.W. in a court of public opinion that they, and the Lady Gatorettes, knew about the illegal shenanigans of Hubba Bubba's Fish camp and were involved in it.

I vaguely wondered if we pushed him into the flamingo pond if they would eat him. Probably not. The foul taste of deceit would conceivably make them puke him up.

Mary Jane, Myrtle Sue, and Flo were straining to hold Rhonda Jean back from killing Hubba Bubba right there on the spot. She was dragging them with her and shouting borderline obscenities. Her strength must come from all the pizzas and doughnuts she consumed.

Misty Dawn was exceptionally quiet. Oh, this was never a good thing. She held up her hand, "Rhonda Jean, this is a code one."

I didn't know what a code one was, but I was going to take my cue from the girls. I was standing next to Misty Dawn waiting to see if she was going to order Hubba Bubba's death.

Flo appeared to ignore Misty Dawn's order, marched over to Hubba Bubba and slapped him in the face. He drawled, "Darlin' you need to do better than that."

Misty Dawn went over and touched Flo on the shoulder. "I said code one."

Flo glared at Hubba Bubba who had a gotcha pose and then turned walking back to the parking lot.

He whistled at her. Never once breaking her stride, Flo gave him a three-finger salute.

Misty Dawn gave a slight nod and the girls went to work, flipping over tables, chairs, anything not nailed down on the deck.

Hubba Bubba just laughed, "That's easy enough to clean up. I had heard you gals weren't good sports about much of nothing."

Marching with the girls into the actual restaurant to do more decorating, I hadn't noticed that Myrtle Sue pulled two cans of day-glow yellow and green paint out of her purse. In fact, I hadn't even noticed she had been carrying a purse, so much for my observational skills.

She tossed one to Rhonda Jean and they both proceeded to spray paint the walls, the tables, chairs, anything the paint mist could land on. Patrons were scrambling to get away from what they thought were vandals. Nope, just some seriously ticked off hormonal women who had not had any doughnuts in hours.

Mary Jane was flipping over tables and chairs as well as throwing dishes down on the floor.

Oh, did I mention Misty Dawn had locked the door when we came in? People could leave but they couldn't come back in...including Hubba Bubba who was out on the deck, pounding on the door, shouting some very not nice things about us, and questioning our ancestry.

The waitresses were all huddled back at the kitchen door. I walked over to the servers in the midst of this mayhem and commotion.

"Yeah?" Jennie was wary. Honestly, I didn't blame her one bit. The Lady Gatorettes were destroying the restaurant. Flo had been the distraction needed so we could do our damage to the deck tables and chair while getting closer to the restaurant door.

I handed each one of the five servers a large crisp bill with a smiling fat man on it. Yes, everyone received the same denomination as Jennie had earlier.

Each one thanked me. Even though they were going to have to clean up the mess we were creating, at least they were being compensated well for it.

The spray paint, on the hand, was going have to be professionally removed. The walls might even need to be totally repainted.

We left through the kitchen's back door, got in our trucks, and left.

Giggling as I left the parking lot, I received a text from Misty Dawn. "Babes."

I'm guessing we needed to warn Miss Lexi, Miss Diamond, and Miss Pinki that Hubba Bubba might have had something to do with Trixie's short life and they should probably re-think the length of time they were going to be performing at Babes, Babes, and More Babes.

We arrived a little early before the dancers did their routines. The two girls twirling on the stage pole weren't very good; however, we did applaud enthusiastically while throwing dollar bills up on stage.

Tommy, the greasy manager, wasn't real happy about seeing six women cheering on the dancers but since we were spending money on drinks, okay it was Coke but whatever, and tossing money at the gyrating honeys, he couldn't complain much.

On a side note, I never did ask why the Lady Gatorettes why they kept a bank bundle of fifty one-dollar bills in their purses.

They were making it rain for the dancers with dollar bills fluttering about on the stage.

Mary Jane waved for Tommy to come a little closer to us. "Who owns this place?"

Little narrow beady eyes just stared at her giving no indication he had even heard her.

"What about a little incentive?"

"Lady, you could pay me a hundred dollars and I still couldn't tell you because I don't know. A CPA comes in here on Fridays, hands me the checks for everyone, and leaves."

Knock me over with a pink flamingo feather! It never occurred to me that Joe D. was doing their books and could probably tell me who actually owned this dive.

Rhonda Jean looked over at me. "Yeah, it's probably Joe D., you need to talk to him."

"Parker and Joe D. sitting in a tree k-i-s-s-i-n-g. First comes love, then comes marriage, then comes a baby in a baby carriage." Mary Jane was doing a sing-song version of the old nursery rhyme.

I clamped down on my jaw, gritting my teeth, and growled, "Shut up if you value your life, Mary Jane!"

She merely grinned.

Miss Pinki was standing behind the dancers' curtain and waved at us to come on back. We trooped back there.

To be honest, it was pretty dismal. Dim lights around mirrors that had probably been there since the 1960's, wobbly wooden chairs pulled up next to the makeup counters that might have been varnished at one time but were no longer shiny except with cheap makeup smudges all over it.

The girls were putting their stage makeup on. We told them everything that had happened with Hubba Bubba. They eyed each other.

Finally, Miss Diamond spoke, "I'm thinking it's time we call it a night. We have enough info for our papers."

Miss Pinki agreed. "If we leave now, it's only going to take about an hour to pack our things up and go back to Gainesville.

"Hubba Bubba doesn't know where you live, does he?" asked Flo, peeking her head around the curtain.

"Unless Hubba Bubba followed us home one night and we didn't notice him, he doesn't have a clue."

Misty Dawn stuck out her hand. "Ladies, it's been a pleasure knowing you and if we can help you in any way, you can text Rhonda Jean."

She nodded her head. "Yep, I have their real numbers and they have my and Myrtle Sue's private numbers. We're good."

I nodded out to the big room. "Do you need to let Tommy know?"

Miss Lexi, Miss Diamond, and Miss Pinki looked at each other before Miss Diamond said, "I'll get him to come back here and then all of us," she pointed at us, "can leave at the same time. The only thing he's going to do is rant and rave at us."

Miss Pinki giggled, "Not like that's the first time either."

Miss Diamond stuck her head through the curtains and did a finger wave for him to come back.

"Yeah." He was just the epitome of good manners, not.

"We quit."

He shrugged. "So what? You ain't getting your last paycheck either." With that he left.

"For a buck two ninety-eight, it's not enough to write home about," opined Myrtle Sue. Everyone agreed.

They grabbed up their belongings, opened the back door cautiously, and then pulled it closed quickly.

"What?"

"Rhonda Jean, you check but I'm pretty sure that's Hubba Bubba standing out there." Miss Lexi sounded a wee bit nervous.

Misty Dawn rolled her eyes and opened the door. "Give him a minute to finish doing his thing and we can leave but we're going to need to hustle especially if he knows what time y'all start dancing."

"Tommy will tell him the minute he comes in the door that we quit," said Miss Diamond. She sounded a little concerned.

Misty Dawn opened the door again. "He's gone and we need to go right now!"

We all ran out to our respective vehicles and jumped in. However, I noticed Rhonda Jean had stopped by a dark blue SUV and seemed to be having a problem because she was leaning over with a hand on her knees.

I rushed over to her. "You okay, girl?"

"Oh, yeah, I heard a hissing sound over here and wanted to make sure it wasn't an injured animal."

It took me a moment to realize she had a tire pressure gage in her hand and was using it to let the air out of Hubba Bubba's tires.

Being a fine, upstanding member of the Lady Gatorettes and in a show of solidarity, I went around to the other side of his SUV, unscrewed the tire caps, and used my key on the tire stem to deflate the tires on that side.

We almost got caught because that low down, rat son of a motherless goat, ran out of the front door of Babes shouting and looking around the parking lot.

Rhonda Jean and I were already crouched down so he couldn't see us. We ended up doing the crab walk behind other vehicles to reach our trucks.

"Hey, I whispered, "I'm going to throw some of this gravel over to my left, when he starts heading that way you hop in your truck and leave."

"I'm not leaving you here."

"Rhonda Jean," I was quiet, "I can get in my truck faster than you. If one of us is going to be caught, I'd rather it be me."

She almost stood up straight to confront me. "You saying I'm fat?"

I groaned inwardly. I did not want to have an argument with her in the middle of a strip joint's parking lot when we've just let the air out of a well-known businessman's vehicle.

My head started to hurt because that nasty little hamster was jumping up and down on his teeny tiny little wheel in my head. I could only surmise he was agreeing at my poor choice of words with Rhonda Jean.

"No, no, no! That wasn't what I meant," I was hastily trying to cover my faux pas. "I meant your truck doesn't have the interior lights come on when you open the door. Mine does. Hubba Bubba won't be able to see you, but he'll be able to see me. At least you can get away fast."

"Oh. Okay." Then, "You need to turn yours off from here on out."

Yes, I probably did except I sometimes dropped the keys in my vehicle even in broad daylight and I wanted to be able to find them when I was not in a full-blown panic mode of doing something perhaps diabolical with the girls, especially at night.

"Ready, set, go!" I threw a handful of gravel away from Rhonda Jean's truck, hitting several vehicles and setting their alarms off.

I swear I didn't mean to set the alarms off. Who knew men visiting strip clubs would have their vehicle alarms still activated while they were inside? I certainly didn't.

However, Hubba Bubba started running to the car alarms probably convinced that either the dancers or the Lady Gatorettes were trying to elude him. Rhonda Jean jumped in her truck and pealed out of the parking lot. I hopped in my SUV and left as well. I did not sling gravel as I was leaving.

Glancing in my rear-view mirror, Hubba Bubba didn't even notice two vehicles had left the parking lot. He was busy circling cars trying to find us.

CHAPTER 17

I strongly suspected the girls were at my house ready to discuss today's latest escapades. I was right.

What I didn't expect was Miss Lexi, Miss Diamond, and Miss Pinki being there.

Do I dare mention the pizza delivery guy showed up at the same time I did?

"You know he is a worthless piece of..." Flo started to say and she was furious.

"Stop!" commanded Misty Dawn holding up her pizza slice. "Parker."

Rut row, she was calling me out by name. "Have you heard anything from Missy yet on Babes' owner?"

Shaking my head no. "Um, can I eat some pizza first?"

She eyed me like she had seen the Loch Ness monster. "What? You can't do two things at one time? Everybody else here can."

Okay, I'm not voting for her as Miss Congeniality this week. Swallowing a large bite, I called Missy.

"Do you know what time it is?" She sounded a little gleeful.

"Do you know I haven't heard from you with the information I needed?" I snorted.

"Yes, and that's because there are twenty-six corporations between Babes and the actual owner." She paused.

"Do you think you could share the love with us on this or am I going to have to pull it out of you?" I groused while trying to take another bite of pizza.

She was being coy. "Who do you think it is?"

"Oh, for garden seed, Missy!" I exploded and not bothering to pick up another slice. "For all I know, it could be the three dancers here or even Trixie. I don't know!"

Rhonda Jean mumbled around a mouth of pizza. We looked at her. Swallowing, she said, "Missy, I'm guessing it's the same ones I finally figured out."

"Probably." She paused for dramatic effect...or that's what I assumed anyway.

"Missy," I growled.

"Okay, Parker, here goes. Babes, Babes, and More Babes is actually owned by Brandi-Lynn Hennessy."

You could have heard a pin drop. We all stopped with a slice of pizza halfway to our mouths when Missy dropped that information bomb on us.

Myrtle Sue asked, "Is this the same Brandi-Lynn Hennessy who was just sprung from jail and is now running for Po Ho mayor?"

"Yes."

We turned to peer at Rhonda Jean who nodded yes while reaching for another slice of pizza.

"How did the FBI and the State of Florida miss this vital piece of information?" Mary Jane was puzzled. "Seems to me three things. One is Brandi-Lynn is a lot richer than anyone suspects. Two, why is she running for mayor? Third, I'm betting she's used Joe D. to launder her money offshore."

They did the exorcist head whipping exercise to gape at me.

"Stop!" I held up my hands. "I've been here with y'all. When have I had any time to call or text Joe D.? Missy, what else do you have?"

"Trixie's real name is Nancy Ellen Calhoun. She's thirty-four and has an arrest record as long as your arm. She's been arrested multiple times for various things. However, she's never been arrested for prostitution which I would have suspected.

"As far as I've been able to find out, she's been in the entertainment industry..."

We all coughed including the dancers. Missy continued, "Since she was about sixteen or seventeen years old. It doesn't appear she graduated high school. That being said, she did really well in her classes before dropping out of school."

The dancers glanced at each other before Miss Lexi volunteered, "She seemed more street smart than book smart."

"But if she'd been dancing for a really long time, street smarts are what kept her alive and making money," mused Flo. "You really can't fault a girl for that."

Miss Diamond agreed. "Depending on the club, you can make really good money dancing and it's hard to let go of a good income stream.

"Also, if she never graduated high school, it's going to be very difficult for her to get a good paying job somewhere. I can understand why she was doing what she was doing."

"Missy, do you know if she knew Hubba Bubba from South Florida or did she only know him from here?"

"That I don't know, Parker. But I do have another interesting big of news for you." Missy stopped for a moment, "Rhonda Jean, do you know about it?"

She had another slice of pizza in her hand. I glanced at her empty box and realized she had misappropriated a slice from my box. Taking a deep breath and letting it out slowly, I stared at her until she noticed I knew what she had done. I arched both eyebrows and pointed my finger at her.

"Yeah, thanks, Parker. I was really hungry." Saying loudly for Missy to hear on the phone, "Probably not. Brandi-Lynn's info was all I had found. What's yours?"

To be honest, we were paying attention but not with every fiber of our being. Remember, there was pizza to be consumed.

"Brandi-Lynn danced with Trixie in..."

Exclamations of "Whoa!" "Shut the front door!" "Are you flipping kidding me?" were heard from the girls and the dancers.

Holding my hand up for silence, I queried Missy again. "Do you have photos, advertisements, anything as proof?"

Misty Dawn chimed in, "Missy, it's Misty Dawn, why hasn't the FBI or the state found out this about Brandi-Lynn?"

"First things first, ladies. Yes, I do have some photos of both of them dancing and being promoted on a flyer. They were very young, but they are very recognizable. I also ran them through facial recognition software and it's a perfect match for both of them.

"Misty Dawn, to answer your question, I'm surmising that once the FBI, the state, local law enforcement, reporters, and whoever else did some background research and found five different corporations that spidered off into a lot of other companies, it no longer was an issue or of interest because they already had Brandi-Lynn on the other charges. Basically, everyone just stopped checking."

"What is the background on her? I don't really know." Mary Jane smacked Rhonda Jean's hand for trying to reach out and capture her last remaining slice of pizza.

They stared at each other before Rhonda Jean announced she might be full, for a little while.

As far as I was concerned that was adequate enough warning to make sure I finished eating my pizza.

"She was born in Fort Lauderdale and moved to Jacksonville, allegedly, when she was in first grade. DCF took her away from her mother, no father in the picture, and she ended up in foster care. She bounced around in the system for a while and then left it when she was in high school, probably as a sophomore.

"Everything indicates she was a really good student. She probably would have done well in school or college had she had any real support growing up."

"Missy, how did she end up dancing and how long did she do it?" Inquiring minds were trying to piece together everything.

"That I don't know, on the dancing part that is. Brandi-Lynn's stage name was Cashmere. From everything we could find she danced for about a year. She came back to Jacksonville and got involved in various community activities and you know the rest.

"Oh, yes, one last thing. She had married a guy near Orlando. His name was Ralph James. He owned a horse farm, and it was rumored that he was selling horses but then not delivering them. He was found dead in his barn about nine months after they were married. The medical examiner's report said he had a heart attack. Brandi-Lynn sold the horse farm.

"He was fifty-five and the marriage certificate says she was twenty-one. I did the math. She was probably eighteen."

"Um."

"No, Misty Dawn, I don't know how or where she met him. In fact, you have to do a very in-depth search to even find this much out. Her official version is she has pulled herself up by the bootstraps and become the All-American success story until the powers that be didn't want a real female success story. There's still a lot of unanswered questions on her."

"Thanks, Missy, that's been a big help. Catch up with you later." I punched the off button.

I looked around the kitchen at everyone. "What do y'all think?"

Miss Diamond smoothed her hands through her hair. "Sounds like she and Trixie both had a horrible upbringing, and they survived the only way they knew how."

"Yes, I'm sure they both have a lot of trauma and psychological damage," stated Miss Lexi who was looking protectively at her pizza box.

Flo popped up with, "Now we know why Brandi-Lynn is in Po Ho even though she can't let the public know that's the reason why."

"Y'all, something else is at play here." Rhonda Jean was tapping on her phone again. She possessed a certain master strategist gene that the rest of us didn't seem to have. Sometimes it was a wee bit off-kilter, but it did give us cause for thought.

"It's bad enough that low down, son of a motherless goat played us..."

I interrupted her. "Rhonda Jean, I don't think he played us on being upset about Trixie. I do think he's genuinely upset about Trixie's death. What I do think he may have played us on are the flamingos."

"So, what do you think there, Parker?" Flo was twiddling the ends of her hair with her left hand leaving her right hand available to slap Rhonda Jean if she tried to snatch Flo's last piece of pizza.

"I think there's a connection between all three of them, Hubba Bubba, Brandi-Lynn, and Trixie. Two of the three are still alive which indicates to me Trixie either knew something she didn't realize she knew, she was possibly blackmailing one or both of them, she was getting ready to boogey on outta here, possibly taking Hubba Bubba's money, or something else."

"Still not adding up," snipped Misty Dawn, glaring and daring Rhonda Jean to reach across the kitchen table for a possible slice of pizza in the closed box that was just sitting there for inspection.

"We know Hubba Bubba didn't murder her," acknowledged Myrtle Sue. "How he was today seemed to be totally out of character for him."

Misty Dawn slammed her hand down on the table making all of us jump. I hadn't seen Rhonda Jean reach for the pizza box, but she could be sneakily quick on snatching food.

"Parker, are you freaking going to call Joe D. or not?"

I tried to glare back at her knowing full well that was equivalent to a six-month-old baby trying to wrestle a steak away from a world-class TV wrestler.

Punching in Joe D.'s number, it went right into voice mail. I shrugged and left a message for him to call me. "He's probably entertaining," I explained.

"If Brandi-Lynn has a lot of money, as I'm expecting she does, why run for mayor here? That's the question that I keep coming back to." Myrtle Sue squinted her eyes. I gave up and slid my pizza box over to her. There were two slices left. Rhonda Jean started to reach for one. Myrtle Sue bared her teeth, "Don't even think about it."

This would be incredibly difficult to explain to law enforcement if they had to come out on how the Lady Gatorettes got into a food fight and a couple of them died. I don't think they'd believe my explanation of pizza slice envy.

"When she got out why didn't she leave the country? She could live a good life wherever and I doubt the government would want her back. She did the crime and did the time. There's something missing."

I didn't disagree. We were missing something. The question was it so large that we didn't have a clue as to or something so simple that we kept overlooking it. That was actually my guess.

Misty Dawn stood up. "Back here in the morning for breakfast. Parker, please try to be up by seven or seven-thirty at the latest; otherwise, half the day is shot."

No point in rolling my eyes or attempting the one eyebrow arch I still hadn't mastered, they'd still be here at oh-hate-thirty in the morning.

CHAPTER 18

Pink's 'So What' started playing merrily on my phone. I groaned and answered it without opening my eyes.

"What?"

"Hey, Parker, need some company?"

It was bad enough the girls were early morning ninjas, but it was even worse when Joe D. called me all bright and chipper.

"No, Joe D., I do not. What do you want?" I was struggling to sit up, move, or get out of bed I hadn't decided which activity had the least amount of movement on my part.

"Love of my life..."

"Stop, Joe D.! You must be single again." Now my feet were entangled in the sheets and I was having a mini-crisis on trying to figure out how to untwist my feet from the bed monster linens.

"You called me, remember?" He was still way too chipper this early in the morning.

"Oh, yeah. Give me a minute." I had finally managed to untangle my feet away from the offending sheets and got up out of bed. I was feeling proud of myself that I hadn't ended up on the floor. "Oh, yeah. Who owns Babes, Babes, and More Babes?"

"Now, Parker, you know I can't tell you that. The CPA code of ethics precludes me from divulging that information." He paused, "However, if you'd like to have breakfast with me..."

Glancing at the time on my phone, I needed to hustle into some clothes before the girls showed up. "Um, can't, the girls are coming in a few minutes."

"Great! See you then."

Pulling the phone away from my ear, I stared at it with complete hate. Not only was it an ungodly time in the morning, the Lady Gatorettes were descending on me wanting to be fed, when didn't they, and then to have Joe D. join us for breakfast was almost too much for me today.

This was starting out of be a crappy day. Even with coffee, I wasn't sure I wanted to engage with anyone or anything. Sighing, I knew I didn't really have an option. Meeting everyone in the kitchen was vastly more tolerable than having them in my bedroom.

I pushed myself to finish getting dressed. Let's face it, how much easier could it be than throwing on some jeans and a Gator tee shirt along with my orange-and-blue sneakers.

Harboring a sneaking suspicion one of the girls, probably Myrtle Sue, was already here and preparing breakfast, I eased my way down the stairs and into the kitchen.

I was right. Myrtle Sue had a big pot of coffee ready and doughnuts on a platter. Tons of other breakfast foods were organized on the countertop so when everyone showed up it was a piece of cake to start cooking.

She handed me a mug. It wasn't until I'd had a couple of sips that my little hamster started his very slow morning routine of putting one tiny little paw in front of the other on his little wheel.

Much like a tidal wave, the Lady Gatorettes burst through my kitchen door. They had enough energy to probably power the entire town of Po'thole for a day or two. This was not conducive to me being a good hostess.

I merely pointed at Myrtle Sue and let her handle them.

Joe D. sauntered in, smiled at everyone, and flirted with Mary Jane. Oh, mercy! If the two of them ever hooked up, I'd move back to Atlanta and let Po'thole dissolve into more mayhem, mischief, and craziness.

Myrtle Sue put platefuls of food out and let everyone help themselves.

Misty Dawn finally pushed her plate back. "Joe D."

He smiled and opened his eyes wide. "Yes?"

"Who owns Babes?"

"Now, Misty Dawn, you know I can't tell you that." He winked and went back to his bacon and eggs.

"How about we give you the information we have and you confirm it. That way you're not technically telling us." Rhonda Jean was trying to see if she could manipulate him. I already knew the answer.

He blinked his eyes.

The girls all looked at me, waiting for the question we wanted to have answered.

"Is Brandi-Lynn Hennessey the actual, real owner of Babes?" I held my breath.

He sat back in his chair and smiled.

Plunging on, "Did you know she was a dancer early on in her life in Fort Lauderdale with Miss Trixie Delight?"

Joe D. was having fun with this. He had a big cheesy grin on his face. The man was totally relaxed.

While we, the Lady Gatorettes and I, wore our beloved orange-and-blue clothing, Joe D. was inclined to look more like a Florida tourist wearing shirts with colors and designs that a freaked out, probably heavily influenced by illegal street pharmaceuticals, clothing costumer had created.

His clothing was garish at best. The crazy thing was as conservative as most CPAs are, he obviously wasn't, his clients didn't seem to care what he wore.

Joe D. was exceptionally good at being a CPA and was nationally known for his offshore banking recommendations on large sums of money. And, yes, he showed up to seminars wearing these same outlandish clothes that we all know no mama would ever dress her child in.

While he gave the impression of being a very laid-back Florida cracker, that was all an illusion. Joe D. was a Type A personality with a ton of drive most Billboard singers would envy. He was worth millions...and those millions were hidden in offshore accounts. Somewhere none of his ex-wives would ever have access to if they even knew about them. I knew for a fact they didn't have a clue about his offshore accounts.

"Did she and Hubba Bubba do business together?" I was still trying to piece together the connections between these three people.

Joe D. shrugged and took another sip of coffee. Okay, if he didn't know that, chances were pretty good Brandi-Lynn and Hubba Bubba didn't.

I tapped my chin, thinking. "Do you now or have you ever done Brandi-Lynn's taxes or bookkeeping?" I felt like I was a prosecutor on some TV crime show.

He smiled. I hated him. Why couldn't he just talk and we could move on with everything?

"Are you going to talk at all?" I was frustrated.

"Nope."

I glared at him, no effect. I don't know why I even try to bother glaring at anyone. I need to come up with a new way of showing my displeasure. Although not mature in the slightest, maybe sticking my tongue out at people would have the desire effect.

"Did Trixie have something on Brandi-Lynn from way back in the day?" queried Rhonda Jean.

A frown creased Joe D.'s forehead. The girls and I did a Gator Chomp. "Go Gators!"

Now we had an inkling of what might have happened.

Smirking, Rhonda Jean continued on, "Trixie somehow recognized Brandi-Lynn and decided to blackmail her for being a stripper. She didn't recognize Brandi-Lynn until she got out of jail."

We focused on Joe D. to confirm Rhonda Jean's hypothesis.

His smile tightened so that it was almost not a smile and he kind of bobbled his head sideways while looking upward.

I snapped. "Joe D., I'm tired of playing this game. I don't understand that last expression. Just tell us what you know. We've already guessed most of it."

"You've done a fair job," he acknowledged. An exaggerated sigh, "Okay, Trixie did have some old flyers of Brandi-Lynn dancing and thought Brandi-Lynn might not want them shown and would be willing to pay for her silence."

He shrugged. "Brandi-Lynn didn't care. Her spin was she had been very young, coerced into doing it, got out, and made herself into the All-American success story. People would pity her and have forgiveness if they ever saw the flyer."

Leaning back in his chair again, he reminded us, "Remember, Brandi-Lynn is very smart. Most people underestimate her."

"Not the government," snorted Mary Jane.

Joe D. merely glanced at her. "The government only found out what she wanted them to."

I was puzzled. "Wait, are you saying she wanted to be arrested and go to jail?"

"Remember, it was a country club type of prison. She could have escaped any time she wanted.

"In response to an earlier question, yes, she has funds overseas. Yes, she could have left the U.S. and lived the rest of her life very comfortably overseas. She chose not to do that."

Misty Dawn had gotten up to get another doughnut when Joe D. started to stand up to leave. She pushed him back down into his chair. "Not so fast."

She sat back down in her chair. "Trixie had to have something else on Brandi-Lynn because I'm guessing Brandi-Lynn is actually the one who murdered Trixie."

"It's possible, Misty Dawn."

I groaned loudly this time. "Are you going to give us more details or not?"

Joe D. sat there for a few minutes. The silence was loud. We were going to wait him out and he knew better than to try to wait me out. He had lost every single time.

Finally he nodded. "Trixie had found out that Brandi-Lynn had been married to Ralph James."

We all shook our heads. We already knew that.

"Ralph had been a very successful horse breeder prior to marrying Brandi-Lynn. I'm guessing she may have met him when she was dancing in South Florida.

"Anyway, he apparently showed her the ropes on how to sell horses and either not deliver them or have them supposedly die enroute to the buyer."

"But did he really die of a heart attack?" Flo was on track with what we were all thinking.

"Well, let's put it this way, that's what the medical examiner's report said."

"Rat poison." Rhonda Jean suggested. "Unless someone is specifically looking for it, you'll never know that is what could have killed someone. Bloodwork shows up as a vitamin K deficiency."

Amazing what these women knew.

"So she killed him." Mary Jane's voice was flat.

Joe D. nodded, "Quite possibly. She had come to one of my seminars right before Ralph kicked the bucket."

We groaned. Yeah, it wasn't funny.

"Anyway, shortly after he died, she came to me wanting financial advice."

Rolling my eyes and shaking my head, I said, "Let me guess, you put her into one of your many partnerships..."

"To which you've made money from," he retorted.

Rut row. Did I have a possible connection to all of this?

Joe D. catching my suddenly paled complexion. "You're safe, Parker. There are quite a few partners in that same syndicate.

"Anyway, she told me she was selling the horse farm along with all of the horses. She was going to have a nice little chunk of change and she wanted it to be protected for her future."

"And, of course, you could help her."

He sighed, "Yes, Parker, I help all of my clients, including you guys. By the way, have you had any response yet on your fancy scanner watch?"

I shook my head no. "Focus, Joe D., and finish up."

"That's pretty much it. I didn't hear from her for years until I saw her on TV about her charges. Did she send money out of the country? Yes, every year like clockwork."

"I'm still confused. Why did she want to get arrested?"

"Myrtle Sue, think about it. The government thinks they've found and gotten everything they wanted from her. They will not continue to look. She looks like a low-level player to them. She's off the hook."

I continued his train of thought, "She's home free on everything that this one," I pointed my finger at him, "helped her to hide from years ago.

"Also, if she left the country right after getting out of a lovely government sta-cation resort, that could set off another investigation and that's what she doesn't want."

"I get it," Flo bobbed her head up and down. "If she runs for office, whether she gets it or not, it appears she's still interested in politics. Being in Po Ho gives the illusion she thinks we're stupid enough to vote her in."

Joe D. smiled. "If she loses, and I don't think she will because no one is running against her."

Seeing us starting to laugh, he questioned me, "What? What am I missing here?"

Sputtering while laughing, I managed to get out, "She has someone running against her, Maisy Byrd."

We could see the rubber burning in his brain. "Don't believe I know her but, hey, she's got a chance. Brandi-Lynn isn't particularly well-loved by a lot of people. I dare say if she loses, she'll disappear from this area within a couple of months."

"Like maybe to a much warmer climate," opined Flo.

"Wouldn't doubt that for a moment." Scanning our faces. "You might want to contact your attorney to see if I need to start finding the best vehicle for y'all to move your money offshore." He stood up. "Ladies, it's been a pleasure. Parker, you owe me lunch."

He left.

"You know all of this makes sense," slowly said Rhonda Jean. "Still, what's up with that nasty Hubba Bubba and the flamingos?"

CHAPTER 19

I groaned. **I hated owing** Joe D. lunch because not only did I have to deflect his amorous passes and profession of his undying love for me, but I also have to keep my own emotions under control. Yes, I still had feelings for him, but I wasn't about to admit that to anyone. I could barely admit it to myself. I'm not wild about my barely controlled hormonal influxes around him.

I called Robert which went right into voicemail. "Hey, it's Parker. What's the status on the watch scanner thing? I need an answer today. Call me."

The girls looked at me quizzically. Finally, Flo said, "You know, if that deal doesn't go through, it's not the end of the world."

Misty Dawn exploded. "Enough of this crap! What's up with Hubba Bubba and those wobbly-kneed pink things at the fish camp?"

"Yeah, speaking of those pink flamingos, what's up with you not liking them?" asked Flo. "No more putting us off about them."

Misty Dawn stared at Flo and finally muttered something.

"Um, what was that you said, Misty Dawn?"

"I got bit by one when I was a kid. I don't like them." Misty Dawn actually looked embarrassed. "Back to the task at hand."

Snapping her fingers, Rhonda Jean smiled knowingly. "Who else has Hubba Bubba had a relationship with? Or, better yet, which one of his waitresses probably has an idea of what's going on?"

Oh, mercy! I could see where this was heading. Better to jump on it now before the girls did their best verbal impression of the World Wrestling Association doing a nosedive move on me.

"Don't even bother," I sighed, "I'll go ask Jennie this morning."

The Gator Chomp made its way back into our daily routine, better known as every opportunity that presented itself.

Pink's 'So What' started playing on my phone. "Hey, what's up, Missy?"

"I think I found the connection between Trixie and Bran-di-Lynn."

"Whoa! Let me put you on the speaker. Go ahead."

"Trixie may have helped Brandi-Lynn kill her husband. There's a very old video of the two of them buying rat poison from a farm store with the date on it from way back when."

"Stop." Rhonda Jean sounded dubious. "Most stores did not have video cameras set up way back when, much less have the capability to keep it on file somewhere."

Missy seemed to agree. "True except what if I told you there was an old VHS cassette tape that has been located?

"It looks like a store employee they were flirting with was the one filming them. Remember, video cameras were a big thing back in the day and the guy may have felt honored to be filming them. Who knows?"

I interrupted her. "Where did you find this tape? Please tell me you didn't have someone in the office create it."

"No, I didn't, Parker. It was found in that box of old tapes you sent us. I had one of the guys go through them and that's what he found."

"Still pretty circumstantial." Rhonda Jean wasn't convinced it proved anything.

"Except it also shows Brandi-Lynn in her kitchen putting the rat poison in a beer and saying, 'this ought to do him in and I'll get everything.' You can hear Trixie off-camera laughing and agreeing with her. Next scene is with Brandi-Lynn handing her husband the beer while she and Trixie were flirting with him."

Rhonda Jean mused, "Yep, that's pretty hardcore evidence, al-though a really good attorney could still argue it's circumstantial. It definitely shows motive though."

Mary Jane added, "Also, shows that Trixie and Brandi-Lynn have had a long-standing friendship. Whatcha wanna bet Brandi-Lynn knew the tape still existed and she wanted it."

"Trixie was pretty savvy on a lot of things. She may have even teased or was blackmailing Brandi-Lynn with it. There is no statute of limitations on murder in the state of Florida. I could see where Brandi-Lynn wouldn't want to go back to prison, and I can def-initely see her not wanting to be convicted of murder." Misty

Dawn was putting the puzzle pieces together. "I have a feeling it was blackmail. Brandi-Lynn may have gone over to Trixie's house to either pay her or try to get the tape back. Things went south and Trixie is dead. Don't think I'm too far off on that."

We all agreed. I was trying to remember if anything was out of place in the house when we searched it.

Myrtle Sue, looking pensive, said, "We went through the house and nothing looked out of order except that one box marked memories in the guest bedroom."

Misty Dawn interrupted her, "Yes, that was the box I opened and saw the tapes in there. Parker had said she was going to send it to her office for them to go through. That was it."

"Brandi-Lynn probably overlooked it. After all, a box marked memories could be anything."

Rhonda Jean snorted, "First thing I woulda looked in."

"Yeah, well, you didn't. Misty Dawn was the one," sniped Mary Jane.

Time to reel them in before anything got out of control.

Missy had been listening to our entire conversation. "What do you want me to do with the tape, Parker?"

Good question. "Um, ask Robert but I'm thinking we just need to hang onto it. Brandi-Lynn's not going anywhere until after the election, so we've got a little bit of time to decide. I'll ask Robert whenever he calls me back."

"He's in court this morning." Missy informed me. We chatted another moment or two before I headed out to the fish camp to see if I could pry any information out of Jennie before Hubba Bubba showed up.

Arriving in the parking lot and managing to secure a great spot in front of the restaurant, I walked in. I was surprised no one cringed when they saw me. My greasing of their palms in a generous way the last time I was in here probably paved the way for me.

Jennie ambled over. "How many of y'all today, Parker?"

"Actually, Jennie," I glanced at the room to make sure it wasn't busy and Hubba Bubba wasn't around, "I want some information that I think you can help me with."

She cocked an eyebrow at me. Why is it everyone can do that but me? I swear there's a conspiracy in the universe to keep me from being able to do that and, no, I'm not going to ponder or ask the esoteric question of what lesson I'm supposed to learn from this. I don't think I really want to know anyway. I think it's more a matter of poor muscle control on my part. Basically, those pesky eyebrow muscles refuse to learn a new trick.

"Yeah, what kind of info?" She was wary. Time to grease the palm generously once again.

"How many times has Hubba Bubba gotten flamingos delivered here?"

She glanced around. "I'm going to take a break. I need to let Nancy know. Meet me in there." She pointed at the meeting room.

A few minutes later, she came in and locked the door behind her. This ought to be interesting.

"Parker, you've always been very nice to me but there's a lot of things you don't know about Hubba Bubba."

I nodded encouragingly. "Tell me what you know and you'll be well compensated."

Taking a deep breath, "Thanks, Parker, I appreciate it. I'm a single mom with three kids and everything helps."

Taking another deep breath and letting it out almost explosively, she continued, "Hubba Bubba is running some type of flamingo scam. Once he hooked up with Trixie things started changing around here. Oh, it wasn't perfect before and we, all of the girls here, suspected he was dealing in some, um, unusual things but since it didn't affect us, we didn't care. But once Trixie got involved with him, things changed quickly."

"How, Jennie?"

"They went to Fort Lauderdale shortly after he started, ah, dating her. A week later a truck shows up with four flamingos in cages in the back of it."

I raised both eyebrows.

"The cages were tall like jail cells, and they had hay and padding in each cage. Hubba Bubba had a fit when the guys showed up and started to take the flamingos out. I heard him tell them they were supposed to take them directly to Jacksonville and not bring them here to the fish camp. They shut the back door and left."

Pausing for a moment, she then continued, "About a week and a half after that, another truck showed up, same thing. This time he shouted at them to go to Savannah."

"It's too cold in Savannah for flamingos," I volunteered. "In fact, even up here, it's almost too cold for them."

She nodded. "There's been a truck showing up every other week."

"How did he get Miss Maisy then?" I was curious.

She shrugged. "He saw her in one of the boxes and liked her. Then he heard for flamingos to be truly happy they needed to be in groups of four and I guess that's the reason why he got the other three."

"Jennie, how many flamingos do you think Hubba Bubba's run through here?"

She thought for a moment, nervously twisting her hair. "At least twenty-four, maybe more."

"Hold on a second." I punched a number in my phone. "Hey, how many flamingos have been stolen from the south Florida area? Thanks."

"Jennie, could the number be thirty-two?"

She shrugged again. "I guess. I don't really know. None of us were keeping close tabs on the trucks, mainly because Hubba Bubba got really nasty if we showed much interest in them."

"Who do you think was the one who came up with the idea of trafficking the birds?"

"Parker, it was definitely Hubba Bubba. Trixie was only interested in his money. She just introduced him to some guys down near Fort Lauderdale who brought them up here."

The last question was going to make me nervous asking it, but, hey, go for the homerun. "Jennie, was he really in love with Trixie?"

Smiling, she answered, "Yes, he really did love her. I think he wanted to marry her. Since she's died, he's been even more short-tempered than normal. And, before you ask, no more deliveries of flamingos.

"One last thing that may or may not make any difference, he was a lot happier with Trixie around even though they had their disagreements."

She stood up indicating our meeting was over. "He seems to have moved on pretty quickly though."

I had already reached into my purse to dispense a decent amount of cash to the beleaguered, working mom of three when she said that. "How do you mean, Jennie?"

"He's dating Brandi-Lynn now."

CHAPTER 20

Blow me over with garlic breath. Hubba Bubba's now dating Brandi-Lynn? Jennie just earned herself a nice big bonus on top of what I was originally going to give to her.

"Say what?" I stuttered. Then horror struck my heart. What if he told Brandi-Lynn Miss Maisy was her competitor in the mayor's race? Would they kill a poor, defenseless flamingo? Little balls of sweat were starting to bead up in fear all over my body.

"Yeah, she came in the restaurant a couple of days after Trixie died. They sat for a couple of hours out on the deck talking. I know he's taken her out a couple of times. Parker, I gotta get back to work." She eased toward the door.

I handed her five large bills. Her eyes opened wide in surprise. "Are, are you sure?" she almost whispered, her eyes becoming shiny with moisture. "That's a lot of money, Parker."

Embarrassed, I didn't know what to say. I was a little gruff when answering her, "Do something nice for your kids, something fun. Thanks for the info."

Nodding, she walked out the door, and then stuck her head back in. "He's not here so you can leave safely."

Arriving back at my house and walking into the kitchen what did I spy with my little eye? Why more pizza boxes. What else would be in the kitchen?

"Y'all ain't gonna believe this," I announced reaching for the pizza box with my name on it. I proceeded to tell them everything Jennie had told me.

"Do you think he's going to tell Brandi-Lynn about Miss Maisy?" Myrtle Sue sounded glum.

"He's not."

I turned my head to look at Rhonda Jean. "What makes you think that?"

Misty Dawn swallowed around a big bite of pizza, "Logic. If she came to him, and it sounds like she did, she probably wants to find out if he knows anything about Trixie's tape."

"The second thing is if he told her Miss Maisy is running against her, then she would have no need to keep seeing him," continued Myrtle Sue licking pizza sauce off her fingers, "and I'm guessing she wants to keep seeing him for whatever reason, probably money."

"Yep, the number three reason is if she loses, she can disappear into the very warm atmosphere of the Caribbean and not have to worry about anything ever again." This was from Flo who was debating about eating another slice of pizza. "Also, if he told her about Miss Maisy, then that means Hubba Bubba would be running Po Ho and that would kill off their dating life faster than a cockroach running across the floor when the lights get flipped on."

Oh, yay, that was a visual I didn't want to think about. I know it's Florida, and I do have a regular pest control service that comes to my house, but cockroaches have been known to survive and thrive in the hostile environment of bug spray. I just didn't want to find one of those nasty critters in my bathroom late at night when I flipped on the light switch.

"There's a fourth reason." Rhonda Jean held a slice in each hand. "I'm taking bets that Miss Maisy wins and becomes mayor. Brandi-Lynn and Hubba Bubba take off for the Caribbean together within two weeks of the election, and one of us ends up getting Miss Maisy." She laughed, "So we'll end up running Po Ho and that ought to send Miss B.P. Harris and her chamber into mental health counseling for sure."

Wicked gleams of undisguised merriment lit up their eyes. May God have mercy on the souls of the citizens of Po Ho if that happened.

Robert called just as we were contemplating the strong possibility of our entering the political arena through a flamingo proxy.

"Hey, Parker, the watch scanner project is a go. It's the number we discussed."

"Wait, Robert!" I almost panicked thinking I hadn't asked for enough money.

He laughed. "Stop worrying, Parker. You did ask for enough money. We spent two hours going back and forth before I told them your number was the only price you were willing to take. If they weren't willing to pay it, then I had a company in Germany who was. That's what closed the deal. Tell Joe D. we're closing next week, and he needs to move the money right then. We don't want any hiccups."

I told the girls we were now going to be multi-millionaires and I texted Joe D. the information. I received a thumbs up emoji from him.

Mary Jane wasn't that impressed about the millionaire part. "So what? We're already multi-millionaires. Joe D. has invested most of our money overseas."

Ah, the joys of a reality TV show still paying residuals. So glad we weren't doing that anymore.

Myrtle Sue had been quiet, I could tell she was pondering something.

"What's up, Myrtle Sue?"

"Who do you think we should tell about the flamingos? After all, they'll freeze to death anywhere north of here. I just don't think that's right."

As true animal lovers, we all nodded in agreement. Then I made a very stupid suggestion. Trust me when I say it takes true talent and skill, which I apparently have plenty of, to make a brainless proposition to the girls. Yeah, I didn't think it through before the words escaped through my lips. "Maybe we should get Denny to go kidnap the flamingos and deliver them back to the original owners in South Florida."

Misty Dawn, ever the subtle one in the group, roared, "Have you lost your ever-loving, freaking mind, Parker Bell? Seriously, what is wrong with you? You're just asking to have all of us arrested. Denny would get John Boy, Big T, and J.W. involved....no, no, no, ain't happening. You just march yourself out to the pool deck, jump in the pool if you need to, but don't come back in here until your common sense is working again."

"Um, you realize this is my house, don't you?" I replied weakly. And that's when I felt a laser beam of energy zoom right through my body. I looked down at my chest to make sure there wasn't a hole with light shining through. Misty Dawn's eyes had a strange glow to them and that's the last thing I remember before everything swam in front of my eyes, color ceased to exist, and everything turned black.

I woke up lying on my cold kitchen floor. It was still daylight. I wasn't sure what happened or how long I had been unconscious.

The bad part was the girls were giggling and alternating between high fiving each other and doing the Gator Chomp. I wasn't sure what that meant.

I struggled to get up. Let me point out, not one of my darling Lady Gatorettes offered to help me to my feet.

"New world record, Misty Dawn, ten minutes." Rhonda Jean sounded impressed. I wasn't. That was ten minutes of my life I was never going to get back again.

Finally standing erect again although a little wobbly, I asked, "What was that, Misty Dawn?"

"A new technique I've been working on." She was very nonchalant about it. Other than the fact that she accomplished some new magic trick on me, which I wasn't overly thrilled about since it was on me, I was impressed. I hesitated to ask her if I could learn it. It might not be for mere mortals such as myself. I'd ask her later.

"While you were busy taking a nap, we called the Florida Wildlife Commission folks, told them about the flamingos being trafficked from South Florida to places north of the Florida-Georgia line. They were very appreciative of our being fine, upstanding citizens."

"You didn't..."

Flo purred her answer, "We did mention names but, as we all know, it's going to take some time before they can put together enough proof to arrest Hubba Bubba."

"You know it doesn't pay to aggravate us," laughed Mary Jane. "Payback is heck."

I nodded, ostensibly at what I had just experienced. My little hamster, a little slower on his teeny tiny little wheel, was dissipating the cobwebs that had formed while I was laying unconscious on the kitchen floor. It suddenly occurred to me what they were doing. I started to laugh.

"Y'all are brilliant. When's the election?"

Smiles split all of their faces.

"Next Tuesday."

CHAPTER 21

Listening to the radio on Tuesday night for the election results, we were all in a jubilant mood.

The radio announcer was reporting on all of the races. Making mention of the Brandi-Lynn and Maisy Byrd mayoral race, he commented, "The mayor's race has been very unusual, to put it mildly. In all of my years reporting election results, I have never seen where a convicted felon, Brandi-Lynn Hennessy, could run for office. Not only is Brandi-Lynn hoping for a win in Po'thole but she has spent a lot of money on campaigning with signs up everywhere, radio spots on our station, and newspaper ads. She's serious about wanting to be mayor.

"On the other hand, Miss Maisy Byrd has spent no money on her campaign. Nada, zip, nothing and the informal rumor on the street is she will win and become mayor. Very little is known about Maisy other than what was listed on her application sheet filed with the supervisor of elections."

He chatted on another few minutes and then said, "Brandi-Lynn Hennessy has just entered the elections office, waving and smiling at the folks waiting on the results. Those should be coming in very shortly. She is being escorted by Hubba Bubba Skinner."

Punching each other in the arm and grinning like we had won the lottery, we almost dared not to exhale.

"Brandi-Lynn, Brandi-Lynn, would you care to make a statement for our listening audience?" breathlessly asked the announcer.

"Sure, um, I didn't get your name. Thank you to all who voted for me. As your new mayor..."

"It's Larry. Brandi-Lynn, the results aren't in yet." He interrupted her.

She ignored his correction and continued, "As I was saying, thank you to everyone. When I become the new mayor, we're going to make some wide-sweeping changes in Po Ho, um, Po'thole."

We looked at each other and rolled our eyes. The woman had hubis you had to admit.

"Thank you, Brandi-Lynn."

She interrupted him, it almost sounded as if she had snatched the microphone away from him. "It's interesting that my opponent Maisy Byrd hasn't shown up. You would think she would come and congratulate me on my win."

Oh, gag me with a spoon! The other Lady Gatorettes looked almost like they were going to lose their cookies as well.

Larry had regained control of his microphone. In a barely contained voice, you could hear the anger, "You haven't won yet, Brandi-Lynn. The results aren't all in."

"The keyword is yet," she haughtily replied. "Oh, look, the results are showing up."

"Folks, the results are coming in. Give me a moment and..."

You could hear the piercing scream through the radio followed by a string of obscenities.

The announcer was trying hard not to laugh. "Ladies and gentlemen, that scream and the words that followed was not from any of our staff members. It was from Brandi-Lynn as she discovered the winner.

"The new mayor of Po'thole is Miss Maisy Byrd! She has won by a staggering eighty-two percent to Brandi-Lynn Hennessy's eighteen percent. The citizens made a clear choice of who they want for mayor. I'm looking around for Maisy, but she hasn't entered the building yet. As soon as we can, we'll get a statement from her."

We were exuberant! We were dancing around in my kitchen with our expected win. It was sweet!

"Um, what do you think is going to happen to Hubba Bubba when Brandi-Lynn finds out Maisy Byrd is his pink flamingo?" shouted Flo as she was doing her flamingo dance hopping around on one leg.

"He's a dead man," grinned Rhonda Jean.

Chapter 22

A week later Po Ho was once again in the national news. Oh, it wasn't just about Miss Maisy Byrd, a pink flamingo and not a human being, winning the mayoral seat of a small, sleepy, rural, Southern town.

Hubba Bubba was found dead the morning after the election. Allegedly, he had consumed a six-pack of frothy adult liquid libations and had passed out in his home.

However, seemingly, before he over-indulged, he left a note saying if anything should happen to him, the Lady Gatorettes would receive ownership of Miss Maisy and we could make any decisions on her behalf for the citizens of Po Ho since she was now mayor.

Since mayors can't be, theoretically, 'owned' by anyone, we're just going to let the city attorney earn his keep and figure the legalities out about Miss Maisy's legal guardian.

This, of course, led to speculation Hubba Bubba had committed suicide. None of us believed that for one red hot minute. We were convinced Brandi-Lynn had put rat poison in his frothy adult liquid libations and had probably forced him to consume them in quick fashion.

What happened to Brandi-Lynn? She disappeared in the twenty-four hours following her loss in the election. She's probably never going to be found again in the United States.

All of the flamingos that had been trafficked were located and the Florida Wildlife Commission was in the process of returning them to their rightful owners. Miss Maisy and all of her flamboyance were excluded from being returned since she was now an elected official.

She was also very popular on social media with one hundred million followers and had her own website. Hopefully, her popularity won't go to her head.

We did have to hire security for her and her other pink companions. We also employed the same social media company who handled all of the Lady Gatorettes accounts.

Television pundits were espousing their viewpoints on what was wrong with the South, the state of Florida, and Po Ho, where most of them still hadn't learned how to pronounce Po'thole correctly.

Po Ho would survive.

Life is good.

ABOUT THE AUTHOR

True confession time. I have a wicked sense of humor in case you hadn't noticed. My true desire and hope is I made you laugh while reading this book. My mission is to change the world with laughter one book at a time.

Florida crazy isn't just for tourists, the natives are unique in their own special way. Those zany folks who who live in northeast Florida can't quite make up their minds if they belong in Florida or south Georgia. They do believe in having a good time along with some mayhem, mischief, murder, and wackiness thrown in there. My laugh-out-loud books are clean with no cursing or graphic sex. Read them today!

I grew up in Palatka, Florida, traveled the Southeast extensively for a number of years, and currently reside in Jacksonville, Florida. I decided for my health and well-being it was better to live elsewhere once people in my hometown realized the Parker Bell Cozy Mystery series is loosely (very loosely, according to my attorney) based on them.

When I'm not doing my favorite thing...writing...I enjoy walking my little rescue dog, traveling, reading books, and cracking my friends up with funny stories and my sense of humor.

To join Sharon's VIP Newsletter and to receive a FREE book, go to www.SharonEBuck.com/newsletter.

I absolutely love readers because without you I'd be eating peanut butter and crackers. I greatly appreciate you and your support. The best reward I get is when someone tells me they laughed out loud at my books and that it brightened their day.

People are always asking if I'm available for speaking engagements. The short answer is "Yes, of course." In fact, I can even do a Facebook Live Video or Zoom event for your readers group.

Recommend it: Did you enjoy this book? Please let your friends, family, and even total strangers know about it!

Be sure to sign up for my free monthly newsletter at www.SharonEBuck.com.

Thank you for being a loyal fan!

ACKNOWLEDGEMENTS

T hank you to my wonderful support team and friends for your encouragement, words of reassurance, inspiration, and belief in me on those days when the blank computer screen would stare back at me like a one-eyed monster daring me not to write anything. I survived and conquered.

In no special order, thanks to the following individuals:

Allegra Kitchens – well, she did want to be first since her name starts with "A." Bradley's will never be the same with all of our laughter and silliness with the Cone of Silence.

Michelle Margiotta – Your music has lifted me up when I was frustrated with my writing process, when I had doubts, and it has nurtured the very depths of my soul. Your music is so filled with colors and swirls dancing throughout your compositions that one cannot help but to be totally enthralled and inspired by your incredible gift.

Cindy Marvin – my friend and attorney who tries (hard) to keep me out of trouble before I even get into it.

Southside Chick-Fil-A in Jacksonville, FL – Patty, the awesome marketing manager, and her team who have hooked me on frosted coffee. I am now an addict LOL Every fast-food restaurant in America should take lessons on customer service from them. It's always a delight to go into a happy place of business. I am always treated like a friend, not a customer.

Donna Fucini – There aren't enough words to express my gratitude for your friendship over the years. You are a true friend.

George at Athenian Owl Restaurant – My favorite Greek restaurant and who makes me feel at home every time I eat there.

Steven Novak – my book cover designer who captures my vision.

Nancy Haddock – Thanks for all of the time listening to me on the phone and your encouragement from one writer to another.

And, lastly, thank you to all my loyal readers and fans. I love and appreciate you!

To God be the glory.

Printed in the USA
CPSIA information can be obtained
at www.ICGtesting.com
LVHW010320150524
780350LV00020B/323